CHEWING the SEATBELT

ANDREW DADDO

WALKER BOOKS
AND SUBSIDIARIES

LONDON • BOSTON • SYDNEY • AUCKLAND

This is a work of fiction. Names, characters, places
and incidents are either the product of the author's
imagination or, if real, are used fictitiously.

First published by Hodder Headline Australia Pty Ltd

First published in Great Britain 2004 by Walker Books Ltd
87 Vauxhall Walk, London SE11 5HJ

2 4 6 8 10 9 7 5 3 1

Text © 2001 Andrew Daddo
Cover illustration © 2004 Sue Mason

The right of Andrew Daddo to be identified as author of this
work has been asserted by him in accordance with the
Copyright, Designs and Patents Act 1988

This book has been typeset in Stone Informal and Gothic Blond

Printed in Great Britain by Cox & Wyman Ltd, Reading, Berkshire

British Library Cataloguing in Publication Data:
a catalogue record for this book
is available from the British Library

ISBN 1-84428-648-7

www.walkerbooks.co.uk

For Felix, Anouk and Jasper Sass.

And Jac. I love our family. It's ace!

Contents

Chocolate Cars

There's an art to eating a chocolate bar. A lot of people think that there isn't, but they're wrong. I learned it from the master, my brother: the smarmiest, greediest, most cunning chocolate bar eater in the world.

On the television ads they make it look simple, but it's not. It's complex and it shouldn't be trifled with by amateurs either. The world of the chocolate bar is for big kids; little kids just don't know what they're getting themselves into.

I learned how to eat one in the back seat of my mum's car, a silver Holden Premier with double exhaust pipes, rims, slicks and an electric aerial. I don't remember what was more impressive, the aerial or the wheels. I think the aerial: no one else had one like it.

We'd been surfing at Point Leo, on the Mornington Peninsula. The surf wasn't as good as it was at home – the water wasn't as clean and it was much colder. But it was kind of near where my grandparents lived, and that's where we went for half of our summer holidays. The other half we spent at home.

It was one of those stinking hot days when the northerly wind blows nothing but trouble. I think it was a day of total fire ban, one of those days that made you want to nick a box of matches and light them one by one to see what happened. Mum bought us all an ice-cream and a Mars bar for the long drive home.

My back was sticking to the vinyl seats. My cousin's leg was touching mine so I gave him a slap on his thigh. It was a good one too; my handprint appeared on his leg almost immediately. His family didn't take him out much, so we did. But this was a rule we had and Hamish knew it: "no touching in the car". It was always difficult when you were tired, and it took a lot of concentration to keep your bits to your own part of the seat. But they were the rules, and rules are rules, right?

He bleated an objection, but I said, "Don't touch me on my part of the seat."

"Sorreeeeee!" Hamish said sarcastically. He'd been on enough drives with us to know the rules. He knew better; he knew how it worked. We all did.

My brother sat on the other side of him. Clint hadn't opened his icy-pole or his Mars bar yet. He just held the two of them together, making the Mars bar cold from the chill of the ice-cream. At first I couldn't work out what he was doing.

The traffic was awful. The cars were crawling along and Dad was cursing the scourge of the road, which is what he called caravans. "Bloody caravans!" he said. There was a line of cars that must have been two miles long, and up in front was one stupid caravan, holding everyone up.

"Language," said Mum. "Watch it in front of the children, please."

"Sorry, darl," said Dad. I guess he knew the rules too.

I waited until Hamish had almost finished his icy-pole before I unwrapped mine. It was dripping like crazy. I had to lick it from bottom to top just to stop it from dripping everywhere. Dad didn't like it when we got stuff on the seats of the Premier.

I looked at the seatbelt and the mark was still there. He'd got pretty angry the day I'd done that. I hadn't meant to. I mean, who would deliberately leave their chewing-gum on a seatbelt?

We'd been driving to Yamba in New South Wales for our family holiday. It took two whole days to get there and it was more boring than religious education at school. Mum and Dad used to give us crisps and chewing-gum and sweets to try and beat the boredom. We'd play "I spy" and the number plate game, but that didn't help much. It was still a long trip, and long trips are boring.

I was chewing gum when we stopped for petrol, so instead of swallowing it, I decided to leave it on my seatbelt, up near my mouth. I was preserving the flavour by not chewing it, and I was also reserving my seat for the next part of the journey. Smart. There was no way I was going to sit in the middle. It was too hard to avoid touching anyone. My cousin used to try and get out of sitting there by saying he got car-sick, but he never did, not once. The *dog* did, all the time – that's why we never took him anywhere – but not Hamish. I never saw him throw up in the car, but I used to wish he would, maybe all over Clint.

My sister usually got to ride up front with

Mum and Dad. The old Premier had bench seats, front and back. By being in the front, Elizabeth got to everything first. She got first crack at the sweets, the drinks, and, worst of all, she was first across the border into New South Wales. That was one of the biggest things of our trip. She used to wedge her fingers under the bottom of the windscreen and start screaming, "First in New South Wales! First in New South!"

I tried putting my hand all the way back under the rear window and saying, "Last out of Victoria!" but nobody seemed to care. It was a stupid game; they usually are when you can't win.

We piled back into the car after Dad had filled it with petrol. I started to chew my gum off the seatbelt, but it was stuck. I couldn't get it off.

I picked and chewed off what I could, then flattened the rest down onto the belt, hoping that it wouldn't be seen. I spread it out, trying to blend it with the seatbelt's fabric, but it didn't work. It just looked like a chewed-up piece of chewing-gum, the size of a fifty-cent piece, stuck there. Right in the middle, at throat level. I couldn't even stuff it between the seats. I couldn't hide it at all. I was dead. I spent the whole day trying to chew it off, but it just kept getting bigger and looking worse.

Eventually my father said, "What are you doing?"

"Nothing," I said.

"Yes you are. What are you doing chewing on the seatbelt? Are you hungry or something?"

"No, I just like the taste of it," I offered somewhat lamely.

"Show me the seatbelt," he said, and I did, and he screwed his face up into a thousand wrinkles. He said, "Jesus Christ, what have you done?" He only got religious when he was angry.

Mum turned around to see what Dad was getting so worked up about.

"Nothing," I said. "At least, I didn't mean to."

"Jeeeeeeeeeesus, is that chewing-gum?"

"Yes," I said. My chin started wobbling; I was about to cry.

"Jeeesus wept! How'd you get bloody chewing-gum on the seatbelt?"

"Watch your language, darling," said Mum. "After all, it *is* only chewing-gum."

"Only chewing-gum! God in Heaven, listen to me, darl, do you have any idea how hard it is to get chewing-gum off a seatbelt?"

"You just stick it in the freezer with peanut butter on it," said Mum. She was very practical. She learned stacks of things from lifestyle shows on TV.

"Of course you do," said Dad. "Seen any drive-through freezers so far, darl?" he said out of the corner of his mouth. He was pretty upset.

I kept trying to chew the gum off the seatbelt. "Oh, for God's sake, just leave it. Have you other kids got chewing-gum?"

"Yes," they said.

"Well, spit it out! No, better than that, give it to Fergus and he can swallow it. Maybe we'll all get lucky and he'll choke on it."

I started to cry.

From that day on, chewing-gum was banned, and every time we ate in the car we were not allowed to drop one single thing.

So I was making sure of it with my icy-pole. Not a drop went missing, and even though Clint still had half of his left, I was happy that I would not inspire any further religious feelings in Dad – at least as far as the icy-pole was concerned.

I unwrapped my Mars bar and when I got my hot little hands on it, I found that the outer coating of chocolate was melting. It was tragic. There was chocolate all over my hands and the bar was losing its shape, falling to one side like a half-cooked sausage.

I looked over and saw that Clint had finished his icy-pole and begun the process of unwrapping his Mars bar. He was a genius. He opened one end of the packet and stuck his icy-pole stick into the chocolate bar. He pulled the wrapper off and there, on the stick, was the Mars bar. "A Mars bar pole," he said. "No drips, no mess, just chocolate heaven."

I looked down at the total disaster I had in my hands. It looked like a sloppy dog turd. I rested it on my board shorts, hoping to stop the melting, but all I managed to do was get the chocolate all over my shorts. "*Brrrrrrr-pppppppp,*" went Clint. He was good at making fart noises too.

I looked out the window and watched as Dad passed the caravan. There weren't too many overtaking lanes on this road and he was struggling to hide his glee at leaving the scourge behind. "Cop that, scourge!" he laughed. "I'm telling you, honey," he said to Mum, "they should only be allowed on the road between two and three in the morning, don't ya reckon?"

"Yes, darling," said Mum, sounding like she'd heard it all before. We were going much faster now, and I was hoping the extra wind through the window might slow down the melting, but the northerly just seemed to get hotter.

I was licking my fingers, lips and chocolate bar continuously in the hope of making the thing last as long as possible before I had to bite it. But it was a lost cause. It melted faster than I could lick it and now I had chocolate all over everything. I licked the chocolate off my board shorts, and the combination of chocolate and dried salt from the surf was kind of weird.

What I couldn't reach with my tongue I cleaned with my cousin's t-shirt. After all, Mum and Dad were going to expect him to get mess all over himself because he was only eight, and besides he wasn't one of theirs, so it's not like they were going to kick him out of the car and make him walk home.

I checked on Clint's progress and he was

showing off. He was licking his bar like an icy-pole. Then he made this big dramatic thing about getting through the chocolate casing and into the caramel and soft chocolate below. As much as I hated him at that moment, I had to admire Clint's skill at eating a chocolate bar in the heat. Like I say, he is a chocolate bar genius.

"I need to go to the toilet," said Hamish.

"We'll be there soon. Just hang on," said my father.

"I can't," he said.

"He'll have to hang on," Dad said to Mum. "We've just got past that bloody scourge of a caravan and if we stop he'll get past us and we'll never get to your parents'."

"Can you wait, honey?" Mum asked Hamish.

He shook his head. "I'm going to wet my pants."

"Why didn't you go before we left?" asked my father.

"I didn't need to," he said, and he was starting to cry.

"Jeeesus," said my father. "All right, all right, don't cry. We'll stop."

"Hurry," pleaded my cousin.

"Yeah, righto," said Dad, shaking his head.

I ate what was left of my Mars bar, but it didn't taste as good, all melted. At least I had come second. Hamish had finished his ages ago, but Clint was still going, no drips, no mess. Geez, he was good.

Dad stopped the car and Hamish leaped across me so he could go to the toilet. I gave him a slap on his way past for touching me. He ran to the bushes, pulled his trousers down to his ankles the way little kids do to pee, and waited. We all waited.

The caravan went past. "Caaaaarmon!! Huuuurrry up!" said Dad. But my cousin didn't move. He kept waiting as more cars went past. "Are you going or not?" asked my father.

"It won't come. I can't go," said Hamish. He started to cry. A truck went past. Dad bowed his head, defeated.

Hamish pulled up his trousers and got back in the car. He didn't look at anyone and he didn't speak. Dad put the blinker on, but had to wait for a bus to go past before he could get back out onto the highway. "Jesus," he said to himself.

Clint had nearly finished his Mars bar pole

and had chocolate around the corners of his mouth. He couldn't stop smiling. He looked just like the greedy, smarmy chocolate bar eater that he is and I wished I'd thought of sticking my icy-pole stick in my Mars bar too.

Mum and Dad weren't talking. I think Mum was angry at Dad for being nasty to Hamish. Dad turned up the radio and listened to the footy. It was one of those summer practice matches that don't mean anything. Melbourne were playing Essendon and the Bombers were getting flogged.

Hamish was asleep. His leg was touching mine, but I didn't worry about giving him a slap. If you were asleep you were safe. Mum went to sleep too, and Clint was nodding off, so I decided to rest my eyes as well. It was stinking hot in the Premier, and it felt like all of me was sticking to the seats. Even the bits that weren't touching. I went to sleep and dreamed of a land where all the trees were Mars bars with sticks in them.

Hamish woke me up trying to pull his towel out from under my legs. "What are you doing?" I asked him.

He looked at me with tears in his eyes and whispered so I could only just hear him, "I wet my pants. Please don't tell."

I gave him his towel and mine too, and tried to go back to sleep. Dad would get all religious again if he found out, and I thought we'd had enough religion for one day.

Dead Dog Skozz

SKOZZ

This was the day my dog died. We buried him in the backyard. Dad dug a hole big enough for him to sleep in forever. That's what he said anyway.

Mum cried. I didn't. Dad said he had something in his eye, but I couldn't see anything. I was sad, but not sad enough to cry. Skozzy didn't look sad anyway, not when we snuggled him down in his blanket.

In fact, he looked like he was smiling; he looked peaceful. Skozza looked like he was asleep. Dad said we should all give him a kiss before he wrapped him up to bed him down for "the big sleep". He still smelled the same when I kissed him. He always smelled, and never very good.

Why did he die? I'm not too sure. I know he was very old. I think he was thirteen or fourteen, which is not much different from me really, but it's nearly a hundred in dog years.

My great-grandfather is ninety-three in

human years. He's a bit smelly too, but it's a different kind of smell and he farts more than Skozz ever did. He doesn't do big farts like Dad does in the mornings, but little slippery ones, more like Pop, my grandfather, Grandpop's son. When Grandpop does one of these sliders, he says, "Sorry, son, that one just slipped out...', but usually he doesn't say anything. He just lets them fall out and it's as if the smell hits the floor and explodes like a stink bomb.

Sometimes he blames someone else, or he says, "Who stepped on the duck?" I don't know what that means, but it usually makes everyone laugh. Sometimes he used to blame Skozz. He didn't mind though. And suddenly I knew Skozz wouldn't mind anymore.

I can't remember a time when I didn't have him. He's been here as long as me – longer actually – but how am I supposed to remember any of that?

Dad and I used to take videos of him, hoping that he would hurt himself so we could send them in to *Funniest Home Videos*. Skozz used to love chasing a balloon. We'd throw one up in the air and when it came down he'd try and bite it, sending it back up again. He liked doing that even more than chasing the mower.

This one time, the time we got the video, he was chasing the balloon and the balloon came over to Dad while he was filming. Actually, that's not entirely true. Dad went over to where Skozz was trying to bite the balloon; Skozz jumped up, sending the balloon towards Dad; Dad moved the camera so the balloon would hit it; and then Dad made this big fuss of falling over.

He went, "Oof, ah, oooooooh, wooooaaaa-hhhh!!!" shaking the camera around and finally landing on the ground with a thud. He was hoping it would look like the dog had smacked into him while he was shooting the scene.

We were sure our video was going to win. Dad said it was even better than the dog hurting himself or falling over, because it had a human falling over. "And the one thing better than a dog hurting itself is a dog hurting a human."

We sent it in. Dad got me to write a letter saying what had happened and what Skozz's name was and all that sort of stuff. I said he should be the one to write the letter, but he said it would look better if I wrote it, even though I'm not that good at writing. He said to say I was six, and got me to do the s's and the b's backward, so "dog" looked like "bog".

So I said, "Our bog's name is Skozz."

Dad laughed his head off. Mum said he was stupid, but he said, "Bon't you worry about your mother; it's the bog we neeb to look after..." He just laughed and laughed.

He was certain we'd win. A funny video and a funny letter as well. He worked out where the new telly was going to go, and he was thinking about other videos we could send in too.

But we didn't hear anything from the video people for a long time. Dad said it must have been because they were so happy with our entry there was no reason to get back to us in too much of a hurry. "It's that good, sunshine," he said to me. Sometimes he calls me "sunshine", even when he's mad, but then it goes up at the end, like, "Hello, sunshine." If you know what I mean.

We finally did hear back from *Funniest Home Videos*, though, and Dad wasn't all that happy. The letter said that "humour is subjective", or something like that. It said that some people find certain things funnier than other people, and that they didn't think what we thought was funny actually was. They also gave us tips on how to be a good cameraman, which Dad said was just bollocks, because he'd been taking videos for years. I asked him what the letter meant, and he said, "It means we're not getting a new TV, that's what it means. And it also means that we're not going to watch Kim Kilby in her tight little tops anymore either."

Then he said, "Of course, we could try it again. But this time we'll get Skozz to knock *you* over instead of the camera." He was sure that if he could get a cute dog and a cute kid hurting each other, we'd have a much better chance at winning. But with Skozzy dying, we had to think of a different way to win.

He said, "Maybe we should wait for your baby cousin to grow up a bit until she can feed herself with the milk. I'll unscrew the top of her milk cup and fill it up, but I'll leave the lid loose. Then I'll video her going for a drink, but the lid will come off and she'll be covered in it. What do you think?" It sounded pretty funny to me. He said not to tell Mum, though, because she'd tell her sister and then they wouldn't bring the baby around anymore. It was hard to believe anyone wouldn't think it was funny.

I was going to miss Skozz, even though Mum said I could go and talk to him anytime I wanted. "He's just down in the garden," she said.

It was my job to walk him and feed him, but I knew I wasn't going to miss that. The feeding bit, anyway. He was an animal. Skozz liked his food – more than just about anyone. Much more than even Jason Dowd, and Jason could eat a Big Mac in three bites. (It was messy but he could really stuff it in there.)

To give Skozz his dinner, I had to let him outside first, then put the food in his bowl, otherwise he'd run around the kitchen in circles, yapping and barking until he got it. Once I had it all ready (he liked to have his dry food mushed up with his canned food), I'd open the door and he would run in from outside all excited, jumping up and whinnying like a horse. Then I'd run outside, with him hot on my heels, and I'd throw the bowl on the ground and get out of his way before he ate my fingers along with everything else. It could get pretty scary sometimes. He'd bitten me in the past, but I know he didn't mean to: he was just hungry. He was always hungry.

Once, when we went away for a holiday, we left him with my grandparents. Gon Pop we call them. It's actually Gon *and* Pop, but we think it's funnier to call them Gon Pop. Pop looks like a balloon anyway. Dad reckons someone must have stuck a pump in his mouth, a cork in his bum and blown him up, he's so fat.

When we came back from our holidays, Skozz was fine but Gon wasn't. She was hobbling around on crutches with a sprained ankle and a broken wrist, and Pop wasn't very happy about it. They live in a big old dusty house with skinny little brick stairs that lead from the back door to the yard. And it was those skinny stairs and Skozz that were the problem.

Gon had been getting Skozz's food, but I don't think anyone had told her what an animal he was at mealtimes. She went outside to get his bowl, and when Skozz saw that, he went absolutely bananas. I don't think Gon Pop gave him the scraps off their plates from lunch, because Gon said he was running around the kitchen like a blue-arsed fly, whatever that means. He was jumping up, yelping and barking and just going insane.

She didn't put him outside first, either. She just went right on with the business of smoking her cigarettes and getting his dinner. She always had two "fags", as she called them, burning somewhere in the house at the same time. That way, when she wanted a puff, she didn't have too far to walk. So while she was smoking one of her fags, she made his dinner: the dry food first, then half a can of sloppy, stinky dog food. All the while Skozz was going nuts.

Gon dropped some of the food on the floor and Skozz was onto it like an ant at a family picnic. While he was licking it out of the cracks in the tiles, Gon took his dinner to the back door, the one above the skinny concrete steps, and bellowed, "Skozz, you get OUT of it! Come and get your dinner!" He looked up and saw her at the door, holding his bowl.

She must have looked like an angel to him, standing there in the doorway, the afternoon light streaming in behind her, her white hair glowing, her sun dress billowing in the southerly breeze – and stinking canned dog food sliding down the side of the metal bowl, with the dog biscuits rattling around the bottom.

That's about as close to a religious experience as a dog is going to get. It was just too much for him, and he ran for her like he went after Mrs Johnson's poodle, Pumpkins.

As Gon told it, "He stood for a moment when I bellowed at him. His tail was still, he stopped slobbering and he just looked up at me, like a normal dog would. And then it happened. At first he started twitching and his tail started wagging again. He crouched a bit lower and slobber started to fall from the corner of his mouth.

"'C'mon, Skozz, get outside NOW, it's DINNER TIME!' I said to him. And I said it a bit sharply 'cause I could see both of my fags getting low. And that was it. He launched himself at me. He was like a cat, or like your grandfather when he was younger at the back end of a six o'clock swill.

"I tried to get out of his way, but I wasn't fast enough. He hit me smack bang in the middle of the chest. The dog food went flying all over me, and your rodent dog was trying to eat it straight out of the air. The dog food wasn't the only thing to go flying either.

I could feel myself falling down the stairs. It was terrible. There was a bang and a crash and a thump and *whump*. While the stupid dog was eating the food in mid-flight, I was trying to grab the handrail that wasn't there and the two of us ended up in a terrible mess on the ground at the bottom of the steps.

"I could feel my wrist had snapped. I was covered in dog food and the stupid dog was on top of me with his tail wagging and his mouth slobbering. He was licking his food off my favourite sun dress, which was ruined. Absolutely ruined, I tell you. I pushed him off and tried to get up, but I couldn't, because my ankle was smashed as well. If it hadn't been for all those years playing tennis with the Lions club, I might never have been strong enough to get off the ground and call your grandfather to come and save me.

"It was terrible, just shocking, I tell you. I'm lucky to be alive."

Gon had worked herself into quite a state. She was spitting while she talked and her arms were flapping about as she finished her story. Pop was sucking his teeth and *cluck-clucking*, and Mum just stood there not having a clue what to say.

Dad leaned down to me and said, "Geez, if we'd had that on video we would've won for sure."

And you know what, I reckon we would've.

He was a good dog, Skozz, and I miss him. But like Mum said, he'll always be at the bottom of the garden if I ever need to talk.

Unauthorized Loans

My father's pockets have always made noise. Always. It doesn't matter if it's change or keys or even golf tees. My father has always jangled.

One Christmas I made him a jangle box, somewhere to keep this noise. It was really just a cereal box with coloured paper around it, but I made it and I was proud of it, like I was of my dad.

He mainly used the jangle box for his shrapnel. His keys lived on the hall table. If Dad was home, his keys were there, right where he left them. I wished Mum kept her keys on the hall table, though. She always put them wherever she could forget them, or that's the way it seemed. The same for her glasses and her purse. It was almost like they had legs and ran away and hid from us.

Whenever we were late for school or footy or swimming, her stuff always did a runner. "I can't drive without my car keys and I can't

41

find my keys without my glasses..." she used to roar at us while we pretended to look for her stuff. I made her a string to tie the glasses around her neck, but she said that made her look old.

And I thought she *was*.

After a while, my dad's jangle box became like a treasure chest, filled with a glittering booty of coins and golf tees. Tens and twenties and fifties and dollars, new and old, clean and dirty.

There must have been a fortune in there. I told Dad that. I said to him, "Dad, you must have millions in that box."

He just smiled and said, "Oh, I dunno about that. I don't know how much there'd be, but I don't think it'd be millions. Maybe one million. Maybe only halfa."

Only halfa, I thought, *maybe only halfa*. He didn't even know how much he had in there. If it had been mine I would have known, even if it took me all year to count. But my dad's never been that sort of father.

Like when he sent us down to the shops to get milk or bread or tomato sauce. Sometimes he forgot to ask for his change, and I usually forgot to remember to give it to him, which was pretty much how my piggy bank got started.

I've always thought that if people can't remember to ask for things, then maybe they don't really need them. Like Mum and her glasses and keys. She forgot where she put them but remembered to ask for them when she couldn't find them. That meant that even though she lost them, she really wanted them. If Dad really wanted his change, he would've asked, and he did sometimes, so there *were* days when he actually wanted it.

I thought a lot about how Dad didn't know how much he had in the jangle box. I thought that if he didn't know what he had, then he probably wouldn't know if he didn't have as much as he didn't know he had, if you know what I mean.

Dad had taught me always to test your hypotheses because, as he said, "If you're going to have an opinion, you might as well be right." So I didn't think of taking money out of the jangle box as stealing; I thought of it as part of a scientific experiment. A test, a trial, if you like. If I was right, maybe I'd make some money out of it as well.

Even though I was conducting an experi-

43

ment, it was still important to me that I wasn't caught. That's not to say that I thought what I was doing was wrong; it's just that I knew it wasn't quite right.

The jangle box was in Mum and Dad's cupboard where they kept their clothes. It was on the third bottom shelf between Dad's socks and pants. As long as I live I don't think I'll ever see so many pairs of black socks and white pants. My pants were all sorts of colours, but Dad just had white. White and big; Dad had big pants. "Bogcatchers" is what we called them. Blue-ringed bogcatchers.

I remember when we played World Championship Wrestling, Dad's pants were great because you could wear them as a mask and look through the hole in the front. Whoever wore the pants was the masked blue-ringed bandit, because there were blue rings around the waistband.

I still don't know why we got into trouble for playing with his underpants on our heads, but Mum said it was disgusting and we shouldn't do it. "Underpants are for covering your privates, your penis and your bottom, so unless you want me to call you all buttheads, you'd better keep them off your face." She laughed her head off after she said that.

So the jangle box was between the boggies and socks, which might be why Dad used to talk about the family jewels in play fights. I crept in one day before school while everyone else was busy doing whatever they did to get ready.

I'd already done my jobs, and that included polishing my school shoes. I'd cleaned them on top and underneath, just to show how good I could be in case I got caught with my hand in the box. I'd never cleaned the bottoms before and it was amazing how shiny you could get them.

I waited until there was no one around Mum and Dad's bedroom, walked in, straight into their closet, and just as my fingers were getting close to the opening, I heard my mother call my name. I froze.

"Fergus? Feeeerrguuuss?" she bellowed. "Have you seen my glasses?" I nearly died. If Mum was on a glasses rampage she was going to hit the bedroom in no time. I stuffed my hand in the jangle box, got as many coins as I could, and three golf tees. I put the tees back in the box and put the change in my pocket.

It came to $3.20. A dollar, two fifties, four twenties and four tens. If Dad didn't notice this much missing then he was mad, or rich, or both.

Mum was stomping up the hallway, so I had to get out of their closet and quick, or I'd be caught. Then she stopped. She must have found her glasses so I was saved. They were probably on the hall table. I thought about taking another dip in the jangle box.

She started stomping again, only faster. Then she roared, "Who's tracking muck all through this house on the bottom of their shoes?"

It can't be me, I thought. *Not after the way I've just cleaned them*. And I'd only walked on the carpet since I'd done it, so they'd still be spotless.

I looked down just to check, and there, to my horror, below me and behind me, was a trail of footprints. Black and perfect. Shoe polish prints to be exact, leading right to the spot where I was standing, right into Mum and Dad's closet. Right to the jangle box that was now $3.20 poorer. I was dead.

I turned around, wondering what to do, when I saw my mum's glasses right there between her knickers and her bras. I grabbed them and yelled out, "MUUUUUUUMMMMM, I found your glasses!" just as she came around the corner.

"What are you doing?" she asked, sounding more than a bit annoyed.

"I was looking for your glasses," I said, hoping that the change in my pocket wouldn't jangle.

"What have you got on your feet? There are footprints all the way from the laundry to here. What on earth have you been doing? I thought I asked you to clean your shoes? What's going on?"

"I did; I cleaned my shoes. See? I even polished the soles, so the whole shoe would be clean, see? I thought you'd be happy."

I held up my foot so Mum could see just how good I'd been. She looked at them and looked at me, and looked back at them and shook her head. "Fergus," she said, "what am I going to do with you? You don't clean your shoes on the bottom because, as you can see, you'll leave footprints all over the house. Okay?"

"Sorry, Mum, I didn't know," I said. Maybe if I'd thought about it I would have. It made a lot of sense now that she mentioned it. But Mum had her glasses, and I had a lesson about shoe cleaning and $3.20 in my pocket for my trouble. It was funny how things worked out.

I waited to see if Dad said anything about his box having less of a jangle. In three days he didn't say boo. He kept putting his keys on the table and his noise in the box. Life went on as usual for everyone, except for me. I had $3.20 hidden in a neat little stack under Mum's geraniums, and the newsagent's had the new season's footy cards.

That's how I invested the first instalment of my experiment. Three packets of football cards. That meant fifteen cards and three pieces of fairly flavourless bubblegum. This caper was looking pretty good.

After a few more days, Dad still hadn't mentioned the money, and I decided to make another withdrawal. Only this time, I didn't polish the bottom of my shoes.

It was kind of like a lucky dip really. You just stuck your hand in and waited to see what you got. This time it was $4.35, or four packets of footy cards. If I kept this up, I was going to have a full set before the end of the season. I'd never had a full set before, or so much bubblegum either.

I kept at it too, because Dad never noticed. He never said a thing. I had borrowed enough from Dad's jangle box to buy seventeen packets of cards and a filling's worth of bubblegum. Mum reckoned bubblegum gave you fillings, and I got one, so I suppose that's how much I'd had.

I could have gone on like this forever, and I was becoming more popular at school because I had so many cards to trade. Dad still hadn't said anything about money going missing from his jangle box, so I was right: he really was too rich or too stupid to know how much money he actually had.

As I say, I could have gone on like this forever, and I probably would have, if it hadn't been for my sister. Elizabeth was older than me, quite a lot older in fact. She almost had a boyfriend, almost needed to wear a bra, and had her own subscription to *Dolly* magazine. She also had braces on her teeth.

No one had seen Elizabeth's teeth for almost two years. I wasn't even sure if she had them anymore. The day that she got braces was the day she started smiling with her mouth closed. Actually, the day she stopped smiling with her mouth open was the day *after* she got braces. That was the day we called her "train-tracks" or "monorail" or "tin teeth" – anything like that.

We got in a lot of trouble for teasing her about the braces, and since then no one had seen her teeth, whether she smiled or not. She ate dinner with her lips over her teeth, she spoke with her lips over her teeth, and when she laughed, if she couldn't get her lips over her teeth, she'd cover her mouth with her hands.

Mum and Dad said we would owe them a fortune in therapy when Elizabeth was older, but I never really understood what that meant. The last time we'd seen her teeth they were crooked little things that pointed in every direction. She looked kind of like a shark with gum disease. That's how I remember it anyway.

My set of footy cards was almost complete. Dad still hadn't noticed that his box had a lot less jangle, and if I could have just got my hands on a Matty Beazley, big, fat, sweaty Roger Mound would trade his Benny Niall. My life was nearly perfect, but my buck-toothed, train-tracked sister was about to ruin all of that for me.

I was in Mum and Dad's closet, about to make another assault on the jangle box. Dad had moved it recently from between his socks and pants to his golf shirt shelf. In fact, it was now hidden behind his golf shirts. To get to it, I had to climb up past the pants, past the vests and balance with one foot in the work shirts while I felt around behind. It was becoming quite an ordeal.

On this particular day, just as I had my hand buried in the box sifting out the golf tees, my sister walked into the room and caught me. She looked ecstatic. She had a huge smile on her face and it was the first time I'd seen her teeth in ages. They looked fantastic. They were big and bright and straight and I hardly even noticed that she still had the braces on.

"BUSTED!" she yelled in a state of obvious glee. "BUSTED! BUSTED! BUSTED! BUSTED! BUSTED! SUCKED IN, BUSTED BAD, YOU'RE GOING TO GET IT, I'M TELLING!"

"No, don't! Please? Don't tell!" I pleaded in a weak and pathetic little voice. "Please? I'll be your best friend. I'll do all your jobs."

I was crushed, humiliated. "I won't tease you anymore about your train-tracks, I won't call you "tin teeth", I promise I won't, just pleeeeeaaasse don't tell, please."

"I don't care about my braces," she roared. "They come off on Tuesday anyway, and you are BUUUUUUUUUSTED BAAAAAAAAAAAAADDDDDDDDD!!!!!!!!!!"

"I'll give you half if you don't tell," I offered.

"I'd rather tell," she said.

God she was a cow. I felt like belting her, I felt like all sorts of things, even crying. Elizabeth started laughing and walked out. I chased after her and pleaded with her again.

She just turned and smiled her big straight-toothed tinny smile at me and said, "I'll tell you what, you thieving little rodent. I *am* going to tell on you, but I won't tell you when I'm going to do it. So you have to be nice to me, do all of my chores and give me all the money, or I'll tell right now."

I gave her the money, though I don't know why. If she was going to tell on me anyway, I probably should have kept it. My chance for a full set of cards was fast becoming a dream. And now that I'd been caught, I wouldn't be able to get any more money, which meant I had buckley's of getting a Matthew Beazley card that I could trade with fat Roger for his Benny Niall.

I was devastated. The worst thing was that when Elizabeth told Mum and Dad, I was going to be in real trouble. I sat on the toilet, locked the door and went through my cards again. It was a peaceful place to think about my future.

That afternoon when Elizabeth came home from school, she said to Mum that she had a secret. Mum asked what it was and she just smiled her new and improved toothy smile and said, "If I told you, it wouldn't be a secret, would it?" Mum said her teeth looked lovely.

I was dying, she was killing me, and I had to set the table and wash up and take out the rubbish.

That night at dinner, she did it again. "I've got a secret, I've got a secret." I wished she'd just get it over with and put me out of my misery.

Dad said, "You look very happy with yourself, Elizabeth. Gee, your teeth are good, aren't they? Now stop being such a pain in the butt and tell us your little secret."

"If I told you, it wouldn't be a secret, would it?" she said.

"Grow up and don't be ridiculous," said my father. "You know we don't have secrets in this house."

"*I* do!" she said, her teeth glowing. She was such a pain.

"No, you don't," said my father, a rather stern look crossing his face. "Now what is it that you'd like to share with us?"

I couldn't believe it. Dad was going to make her tell him. I felt like crawling under the table. I wished I could just disappear. I wished I had never experimented with taking money from his jangle box. I tried not to but I couldn't help it: I started to cry.

"What's wrong with *you*?" said my father.

"I've been borrowing money from your jangle box," I blurted out.

"I wasn't going to tell!" said Elizabeth.

"What?" said Mum and Dad at the same time.

"I've been borrowing money from the jangle box," I sobbed. The tears started gushing from my eyes. I was so humiliated I couldn't look up. "I'm sorry, I didn't mean to. I only did it to see if you would notice, and then when you didn't, I just kept taking it." I could hardly speak for the tears that were streaming down my face. "I only wanted to see if you knew how much you had in there."

Nobody said a word. The silence was worse than being yelled at. It was the first time I could recall that my father hadn't made a noise. At least when you were yelled at, you knew it was almost over. But when there was silence, it was all ahead of you.

"Fergus," said my father, his voice deep like it usually is when he answers the phone. "I'm very disappointed in you. I have known someone's been stealing from that box for quite some time. Why did you think I moved it behind the golf shirts?"

"I don't know," I blubbed as the tears just kept coming.

"Mmmmmm? Why do you think I put it behind the golf shirts? Mmmm?"

I said nothing.

"Mmmmmm? Fergus? Mmmmm? Any ideas, Fergus? Mmmmm?"

I hated it when he *mmmmmmed* me. It meant he knew he was right.

"I don't know," I blubbed again. Still

unable to look at anyone.

"You don't know," said my father. "Do you think that maybe the reason I moved it was to hide it from the person who was taking money from it? Mmmmmm? Well, mmmmmm? What do you think, Fergus? Mmmmmm?"

"I suppose so," I sobbed. "I'm sorry, I really am. I gave some of the money to Elizabeth."

Elizabeth snorted and began to protest when my father shushed her with his hand and said, "I'll deal with Elizabeth later. I think we should deal with you now. What did you do with the money? Sweets and crisps, I suppose. Mmmmmm?"

"Football cards," I mumbled.

"What? What did you say?"

"Football cards. I spent the money on football cards."

"How *much* money?"

"I don't know, not that much. I haven't even got a full set."

"Mmmmmmmmm," he said. "Football cards. Hey, there's a top investment!"

Then nobody said anything.

This was it. Now I was going to get it. I'd be grounded for a year, have my bike and skateboard impounded, and have to do the dishes until I was fifty.

In his phone-answering voice my father said, "Fergus, I'm very disappointed in you for stealing from the jangle box. I mean, Jesus, I thought you understood that stealing was wrong. Especially stealing from me."

"Yes, Dad," I offered rather lamely. "I'm sorry."

"However," he continued, "let me say how proud I am of you for being brave enough to admit that you have been stealing. It takes great character to admit when you're wrong, and believe me, in this case YOU ARE WRONG! Mmmmmmm?"

"Mmmmmmmm," I nodded.

"So because you have been honest with me, I have decided not to punish you..."

I couldn't believe what I was hearing.

"Except to say that I want you to go and get all of your football cards, and I want you to get them now."

What did he want with my footy cards? I left the table to go and get them. I heard my mother say, "What are you going to do?" But I didn't hear the answer.

I relaxed. It looked as if the worst of it was

over. I put the cards on the table and sat down. My father, still in his deepest telephone voice, asked me which were my favourites. I pulled out about eight cards, most of them Melbourne players, and placed them on the table.

He looked at me, looked at the cards, then looked back at me. He then slid a pair of scissors across the table and said, "Cut them up."

What? Cut them up? Was he mad? He wanted me to cut up my favourite football cards, the cards that I'd spent the better part of the season collecting and swapping. I couldn't just cut them up, and I said so.

"How did you get the money to pay for the cards?" my father asked.

I said nothing. I was too shocked at the thought of having to cut up my cards.

"Mmmmmm? How did you get the money, Fergus? Mmmmmm? Did you steal the money from me, was it, Fergus? Mmmmmmmm? Now cut them up."

"Cut them up?" I asked again.

"Is there an echo in here? Did you get the money from me? Did you steal it?"

"Yes," I said, fighting back the tears.

"So would you say it was my money that

bought the cards, Fergus? Mmmmmm?"

"Yes."

"So would you say that these are really *my* cards because I paid for them? Mmmmmm?" he asked.

"I suppose so," I cried.

"You suppose correctly. These are mine. But if you can't cut them up, then I think I will. And it will be a lesson to you that stealing is wrong and you should not and will not do it. Okay, Fergus? You will not steal from me or anyone else again." He picked up my Shane Woewodin and sliced his head off.

"Yes, Dad," I stammered. "I'm sorry, and I'm sorry, Mum." I couldn't think of anything else to say.

"Now you may be excused from the table to clean your teeth and go to bed. And if you need money again, ask first, okay? Mmmmm?"

"Yes, Dad," I said, and I never saw my football cards again.

Flying Boggies

This was a bit weird. It was one of those things where you don't know if it's real or not, like maybe you're dreaming. I'm assuming it was a dream, but even now, I can't be sure. God, I hope it was one.

It was awesome. I could fly and my head was the joystick. If I kept my head up, I would go up; if I put my head down, I'd go down. It was the same thing for turning. If I turned my head to the right, then right I'd go. It was like I was Super Mario, only I wasn't in a game; I was flying for real.

I rushed to school to tell everyone about it. I was so excited that I ran the whole way there. No breakfast, no teeth cleaning, no packed lunch; just straight to school to tell my friends that I, Fergus Arnold Kipper, could fly.

Maybe I shouldn't have gone so fast.

When I got to school, people were staring and sniggering. I looked around, but there was nothing funny behind me. I wiped my face, but there was nothing there. What were they laughing at?

I looked down and nearly died. I'd forgotten to get dressed. I'd gone to school in my underpants.

Not exactly *my* underpants. Not my cool ones; not my briefs. I'd gone to school in Dad's underpants. His bogcatchers – big white bogcatchers. They were much too big for me and the elastic was loose at the top. Dad's pants were blue ringers, with the opening at the front. And the opening wouldn't close all the way. My penis kept trying to stick its head out the hole to say hello and I couldn't stop it unless I held the underpants together. That just made it look like I wanted to go to the toilet.

Which I did, but only to be sick.

Louise Bahboon and Debra Overwood, the two girls who I think I might marry, maybe even at the same time, came up to me and said, "Nice pants, babe." It was terrible. Humiliating. My two future wives (not that they know that) just stood there and laughed at me.

I wanted to die. I wanted to get out of there as fast as I could.

I gathered the pants so they were tight around my waist and ran to where the preps and grade ones had assembly. It was the highest point in the school, the best place I could think of to launch myself from.

I ran up the stairs faster than a speeding bullet and, instead of stopping at the top where Mr McRally gave his daily pep talks, I launched myself over the railing with my head tilted back so I would fly away from there at the speed of sound.

And I did, kind of. My head was all the way back and I was definitely going faster. It's just that I wasn't going up. I was heading down, almost as if I was falling towards the ground. And I needed to be ascending, not descending.

I put my head back further, my arms out wider and my hands even flatter. Now I was definitely gaining speed, and I was slowly straightening up, but if I didn't fly soon I'd land flat on my belly in the playground.

"Aaarrgggghhhh!" I roared as I arched my back as far as it would go. I must have looked like a plane wearing pants with half a wheel hanging out and trying to land on its belly.

Whump! I went as I landed on the pavement. "Ow! Ow ow ow ow!" It hurt more than I would have imagined. I bounced and scraped and it felt as if I'd slid down a cheese grater. "OOOOWWWWW!"

I checked myself to make sure I was all right, and basically I was. My elbows were a bit bloody, and so were my knees. My tummy was scratched, but it wasn't really bleeding. The thing that was really starting to sting was my pride.

Couldn't I fly? What was going on? I'd rushed to school to tell everyone how clever I was, ready to show off like a Roulette at an air show, and not only was I grounded, but in bogcatchers with my privates sticking out the front as well.

It was turning out to be the worst day of my life.

I dusted myself off and walked away like I'd meant to jump off the top of the steps and land on my belly the whole time. I saw it in a movie once. It looked kind of cool, which was exactly how I needed to be looking about now.

The bell rang and I went to class. I didn't know what else to do. All my friends were there and they all sniggered at me for being in Dad's underpants. The blood on my knees and elbows had dried in lines down my arms and legs.

Ms Minter, she was my teacher, asked me what had happened. She looked horrified. "Fergus Arnold Kipper, where are your clothes?" she barked as I sat down at my desk.

"Well, you know, it's the strangest thing…" I stammered. "It seems that I forgot to put them on before school today because I was so excited about telling everyone that I can fly." There was a wave of laughter through the classroom.

"And *can* you fly, Fergus?"

"Well, Ms, I could this morning, early. Like really early. To be honest it was so early I may have been asleep, but I think I could. And I was flying in my PJs too. It was brilliant." The class kept laughing.

"What are you wearing now, Fergus?" she asked.

"Underpants."

The class was in hysterics and Ms Minter tried to shush them, but it was no good.

"Are they *your* underpants?" she asked.

"No, Ms, it seems that these are my dad's pants. I would have worn mine, but I must have got Dad's by mistake. I hardly ever wear y-fronts; I usually wear briefs. My favourites are Pokemon briefs. Dad got them from America." It sounded impressive, even to me.

"Ooooooooooooooohhhhhhhh," went the class. No one else had Pokemon briefs yet, not even Gary Blemish, the most spoilt boy in the class.

Ms Minter told the class to be quiet. Gary Blemish kept "ooooooooooohing" and she said to him that if he didn't settle down he'd have to leave the room.

"Bed-wetter," I hissed at him under my breath. He wet his bed once when I stayed the night at his house.

"So, Fergus," Ms Minter said to me, "you thought you could fly, but now it seems that you can't, and you sit here before the class in your father's underpants, with scabby knees and elbows, and I am wondering just what it is that we should do with you."

I didn't know what to say. Everyone was staring at me, most of them sniggering, and I was feeling pretty stupid.

"Would you like to go to lost property and find some clothes to put on?"

"Yes, Ms Minter."

She gave me the hall pass and said, "Off you go. Hurry back."

"Thanks," I said to her, and before I got to the door, I stopped and turned around to face her. I sucked my cheeks into my mouth until they were touching on the inside. It made my lips stick out at the top and bottom and I wobbled them up and down. I looked like a fish. I was being a fish.

In front of the whole class, she asked me if I wanted to kiss her. I nearly died. I didn't want to kiss her; I just wanted to show her my fish mouth. How could she think I wanted to kiss her with it?

"Fergus Arnold Kipper," she laughed. "I never thought I would see the day when one of my students stood at the door of my classroom, wearing his father's underpants with the front open a little, and blowing kisses at me. I am very flattered."

"But Ms Minter, I wasn't trying to blow you a—"

She put her finger to her mouth and shushed me. "Go to lost property and get some clothes," she said smiling. "And Fergus?"

"Yes, Ms Minter?"

It was shattering.

"Next time you want to fly, you might want to reconsider your outfit and try a cape."

I ran out of there before the class had a chance to laugh.

Broometime

The bus finally stopped at a place called Munchies. It wasn't much to look at, but then again, after watching Flabberguts Harvey turn himself inside out trying to fart for the last half hour, I was ready for a change of scenery. And air.

Munchies was a take-away joint, complete with a sign that flashed EATS DRINKS out the front. According to the menu board behind the deep fryer and the grills, they made anything you could munch on and a bunch of things you couldn't. We were all starving. Ms Duncan had given each of us ten dollars and we could do whatever we liked with it. She said it might be a good idea to save a bit for later, but I don't think she actually convinced anyone, especially not me.

I could see hamburgers, fish and chips, spring rolls, dim sums, and crabsticks – all the things we weren't allowed to eat at home. I hadn't even looked at what I might have for

73

pudding, but I couldn't see how a measly ten dollars would get me even close to what I wanted.

There was a bit of a crush at the counter, with the teachers being served first, then the bigger kids, and finally the shorter kids at the back. I was at the back, which either made me short, or tall and wimpy. I was short, but I wasn't wimpy, and I wasn't the shortest either; Benjamin Low was. He was, I think, going to be a dwarf.

My dad has always said that height is relative. "Relative to what?" I once asked him.

"Relative to lots of things," he said.

"Like what?"

"Like the height of other people around you. Like the height of the fence you're trying to peek over, or the height of your parents. It's just relative, you know?"

"Yeah, I guess so," I said.

I suppose I know what he was talking about. And given that there was hardly anyone in my class I could look in the eye, and hardly a fence I could see over, I also suppose I was relatively short. But I was taller than my mum, and I was gaining fast on my dad, who was, even then, about as wide as he was tall.

"Muscle," he still says, patting his expanding waist. "I'm working out every time I lift the fork to my mouth. *Ba ha ha ha...*" he bellows.

He's a pretty funny guy, my dad. Relatively, anyway, compared with other kids' dads. He's adventurous too, always talking about how he's done this and how he's done that, and how we never do what he did because we spend too much time in front of the "bloody Nintendo" when we should be out doing things. *Any* things. "Just get away from the bloody idiot box before you turn into any more of an idiot!"

That was the reason I chose to tell Dad about our new school trip instead of Mum. As I said, apart from being short, Dad's an adventurer, but Mum isn't. It's as simple as that. She likes me best when I'm nice and clean and tidy; Dad doesn't seem to care, as long as I'm not in front of the "bloody boob tube". Although he does spit on his hand and flatten my hair whenever we go anywhere.

When Ms Duncan, my teacher, told my class about our school trip, she said that it would be the chance of a lifetime, a "chance to see a part of Australia only other people who have been there have seen. A real opportunity to see it as it is, before it isn't like that any-more." Whatever that meant. It did sound pretty good, though. Camel rides, fishing, crocodiles that'd bite your head off as soon as they looked at you, and crabs – great huge beasts that lived in the mud and had claws as big as their bodies that would gobble up what the crocs didn't. It sounded fantastic. Nothing idiot boxy or booby about it at all, except for the name, "Broome". The school trip for the year was Broome.

And before we got to Broome, we had to stop at Munchies for dinner. Our camping site wasn't "too far away". It was somewhere near the crocodile farm, but not so close that if one of the crocs escaped it would be able to find us. A crocodile would have a lot of fun in a campsite full of school kids. It would probably go for the weaker, little ones first, filling up on the "tender little nuggets", as my mum called me, before cleaning its teeth with the long, skinny, bony kids.

So there I was, at the back of the bunch, waiting for the fattest, sweatiest man I have ever seen to take my order. Munchie Man. The longer I stood waiting, the redder he seemed to get. I don't think he'd ever seen the likes of Grade Four and Five from the Balgowlah State School before, and I certainly don't think he wanted to again. Flabberguts Harvey was taking his time. He couldn't decide what the best fart food would be: spring rolls or dim sums. He finally settled on the dim sums, saying that cabbage was one of the best fart foods you could get. I knew I could wait to find out.

Ms Duncan had ordered her food and was waiting out the front. I could see her through the beaded curtain Munchie Man used to stop the flies getting into his shop. She looked beautiful. I know you're not supposed to say that about your teachers, but she really did. The way the sun was hitting her, she looked a little bit like Gwyneth Paltrow, especially if you squinted really hard.

She was laughing with Mr Ford, the PE teacher. They laughed a lot, those two; I think they liked each other. Mr Roseman, who was in charge of the older kids, was tucking into a sausage roll, drinking beer and smoking a cigarette at the same time. He was an impressive man. My dad once said if I learned to do one thing properly in my life, I would be doing well. It looked like Mr Roseman could do three, and all at once.

By the time I got to give Munchie Man my order, I thought he was going to explode. His face was almost purple, sweat glued his hair to his head and his shirt was drenched. I asked if I could have a hamburger and he grunted that there were none left. He'd also run out of chicken, steak sandwiches and sausage rolls. I could have anything else on the board that I wanted, as long as it wasn't dim sums or potato cakes. I ordered fish and chips. He said, "Good choice," and I said, "Thanks."

I paid for my order, as well as a carton of chocolate milk, a Mars bar and a bag of crisps. I put them in my bag on the bus for a snack later that night. A midnight snack, if I could stay awake. I'd never been camping before; in fact, I'd never even slept in a tent.

The thought of going camping excited me, but it scared me a bit too. I was careful not to let anyone know, of course. I didn't want anyone to know that I was worried about anything; I mean, nothing seemed to scare anyone else, except Simon Sargood, or "suck-good" as we called him. He was scared of his own shadow. What shadow there was.

According to my father, there was nothing at all to worry about when you went camping; you just had to be sensible.

Dad had told me everything I needed to do to make sure the tent was safe. He said the first thing, always, is to clear the area below your tent, so there are no sticks for you to roll onto and stab yourself to death with in the middle of the night. He said he knew a fellow who had done that. He said, "If he hadn't died he would have been very, very angry with himself for not clearing his site properly."

Dad also said to make sure there were no snake holes under the tent, because they liked to get out at night-time and eat animals like baby sheep, and if you stopped them they'd get angry and eat you instead.

"Why do they eat baby sheep?" I asked.

"What is a baby sheep called?" Dad asked me.

"A lamb," I chuckled. "And they go *baa baa*."

"Yes, I know, and you're a bit old for the animal noise game. But you're right, and we eat lamb, don't we?" he asked, and I nodded because he was nodding and I had learned a long time ago that when Dad nodded, the idea was to nod too, unless he was trying to trick me when I was in trouble. But I knew I wasn't in trouble, so I nodded along with him. I still didn't know what all this had to do with snakes eating sheep.

"We don't eat baby people, though, do we?" he asked.

"Daaaad, that's feral!" I squealed.

"Not really," he said. "And snakes don't eat baby snakes, so imagine that a snake was sitting around our house and we couldn't get out. We wouldn't eat each other, would we? No." I hated it when he started answering his own questions. "We'd *have* to eat the snake, wouldn't we? Yes, of course we would. And that's why the snake would have to eat you if you sat on top of his house. Understand?" He nodded at me with his eyebrows raised. I nodded back, even though I didn't have a clue what he was talking about. There was no way I'd build my tent on top of a snake house anyway.

After clearing the area, he said, "You have to dig a ditch or a trench around your tent. This does two things: it makes a gully for the water to go into if it rains, and up around Broome it can rain pretty hard, and unless you've got an outboard engine attached to your tent it won't make much of a boat. Have you got an outboard? No, of course not! The other thing about the trench is that it stops snakes, because they don't like to go across trenches." Dad said if snakes were meant to, they'd have legs so they could jump; and, given that they were legless, they wouldn't be jumping across any trenches.

I was starting to wonder if I should go camping at all. Maybe it was too dangerous, but if I stayed, I might die from boredom listening to my father. Camping sounded like a better way to go.

"The last thing to do," Dad said, "is to make sure that you tie your guy ropes to trees instead of putting pegs into the ground."

"Why?" I asked him. "All the other kids will have their pegs in the ground and I'll look stupid."

"No, Fergus," he smiled at me. "You'll look smart. If you have your ropes tied to a tree, you'll be able to hang up your pants and socks after washing them. The other kids won't be able to do that, because their pants will slide down the ropes to the pegs. They'll be dirty as soon as they hit the ground. Do you see?" He was nodding again, with his eyebrows up so high they were almost lost in his hair.

"Yeah," I nodded, but as usual I didn't really. I couldn't see why I would want all the other kids to see my pants anyway. He was funny, my dad. But not always funny ha ha. Funny weird.

"And the very last thing to remember when you go camping, son," he was nodding wildly now, meaning he was extremely serious, "is if you need to go to the toilet in the middle of the night, you do it by the tent. Not on the tent, but *by* the tent. Okay?"

"Yes, Dad," I nodded back.

"You don't know why, do you, Fergus? You don't know why you pee by the tent, do you?" he said, shaking his head. So I shook mine too. "I'll tell you, but just this once, so listen carefully. You pee by your tent so you know which is your tent, and you don't go getting into one that hasn't been cleared properly, and, more importantly, so you don't get lost on your way back from the bog. Okay, champ?" He was nodding again.

"Okay, coach," I smiled up at him. When he called me "champ" I called him "coach",

82

because he said he was my life coach, or something like that.

"And what do you do when you get lost, Fergus?"

"I stay where I am when I realize I'm lost, coach?" I said in an asking kind of way.

"Bingo. That's right, you stay put, because when they realize they haven't got you with them, they'll come back to that spot to get you." With that, he patted me on the head, ruffled my hair, clapped me on the backside and kissed me on the cheek. Funny fella, my dad.

When I put the snack food into my bag on the bus outside Munchies, I made sure not to smash my crisps up with the old police baton Dad had given me to hunt rabbits. I wasn't exactly clear how I was supposed to do it, but after the advice on hanging my pants out for the rest of the world to see, I was scared to ask.

A few of the other kids had their food already, and since I'd been one of the last to order, I didn't expect to have mine for quite a while. Flabberguts was showing off to anyone who would watch, eating his food with no hands. He had mayonnaise and barbecue sauce all over his face and there was a dog under the table, foaming at the mouth, waiting for bits of burger to fall from Flabberguts' gob onto the ground. There were seagulls all over the place and Ms Duncan and Mr Ford were giving them crisps.

It was a beautiful spot. The sun was setting over the water and there were camels with red blankets being led along the beach by a lady in the same colour. There were people riding the camels and I wished I was one of them.

I watched as a man came up the steps from the beach with his fishing rod over his shoulder and a huge fish in his hand. It was beautiful, all silver and blue and with whiskers like a dog or a cat. He walked past the front door and I stuck my head through the beaded curtain and asked him what it was. He said it was a threadfin salmon. I thought I might like to catch a threadfin salmon one day, and maybe one day I will.

I went back to the counter and the fat man behind it, hoping that my food was ready. The only person left was Simon Sargood, the scared skinny kid, and he looked like he was going to cry as Munchie Man dripped sweat into his roll, wrapped it up and stuffed it into a paper bag. Munchie Man was really grotesque. He was purple now, and wet, like he'd been caught in a storm. I asked him if my dinner was ready.

"What dinner?" he snapped back at me. His great paw squashed skinny Simon's roll as he gave it to him. Poor Simon ran from the store as fast as he could, getting tangled in the beaded curtain on his way.

"The dinner I ordered before, with all the other kids," I stammered.

"I gave it to ya already," he said, and he lit a cigarette. He ran his words together, and it sounded like "I gave idéeya awlreddy."

"No you didn't. I haven't got mine yet. I haven't eaten anything at all. I put my snacks in my bag on the bus and now I'm back to get my fish and chips," I said as calmly as possible, although I wasn't feeling calm at all.

"You haven't paid for it yet," he spat.

"I have. I paid for the whole lot at the same time, like the other kids, and they've all got their food and I haven't and I'm pretty hungry and we have to go to our camp soon."

"Well listen up, sunshine," he said as a huge cloud of smoke whistled out of his nose. "The grills are off and the fryers are off and I'll be stuffed if I'm turning 'em on again, so if youse want somefingk to eat it's gunna be a roll or a sandwich, and given that all your little mates have eaten all me bread, it's gunna be a roll. And I want to tell you somefingk else, champeen. I'm not very happy aboud it, because you look to me like you've already eaten." He was nodding. It felt like I was in trouble, so I decided not to nod back. "So the only roll you're gunna get, young fella, is a simple one, and you can choose between peanut budder and jam, or both. But that's it."

"Okay," I said, disappointed that I wouldn't be getting the fish and chips I was hoping for.

"Okay what?"

"Okay, please?" I replied.

"No, stuff all that manners crap. Whadya want? Peanut budder or jam?" he bellowed at me. He flicked a light switch next to the grill and the EATS DRINKS sign in the window stopped flashing.

"Jam."

"Fine, jam it is." He set about making my roll. There was butter as thick as cheese, a glob of jam, and his cigarette dropped ash on the chopping block. "Salt and pepper with this, matey?" he snarled.

"No," I said.

"Good choice," he said, wrapping it in paper and stuffing it into a bag. He handed it over to me and asked me again if I'd paid. I said yes and he let the roll go. "Now get outta here," he barked, coming around the counter at me.

I took off, he slammed the door behind me and I watched as the OPEN sign on the door slid to CLOSED.

I turned round to look for everyone else in the fading light, but I couldn't see anyone I knew. There were people around, eating and feeding the seagulls and that sort of thing, but there was no sign of anyone at all from Balgowlah State School. No buses, no teachers, no farting Flabberguts, no nothing.

They were gone. All of them.

And here I was with a bunch of people I didn't know.

If the idea of camping had bothered me, this was worse. It wasn't even as though I had gone and got myself lost either. I was exactly where I was supposed to be. Maybe the others were lost and I was the only one who wasn't.

I looked around the park, checked the car park, the toilets, the beach, the swings, even

Munchies again, but that was dark now that the lights were off. There was no one I knew anywhere, so I was definitely lost and I didn't know what to do.

Then my father's voice rang in my ears. "If you get lost, you stay put, because when they realize they haven't got you with them, they'll come back to that spot and get you." And I wished he was with me to pat me on the head, ruffle my hair, clap me on the bum and kiss me now. I wouldn't be lost if he was.

But he wasn't, and I decided to take his advice. I sat at the table nearest to the car park and ate my jam roll while I waited for someone from Balgowlah State School to come and find me.

I didn't have a choice really, because I had no idea where we were going.

It was getting pretty dark now, too. People were leaving and others were starting to arrive. I just sat and waited.

A dog came over. I'd finished my roll so I had no food to give him, but he still sniffed around. I think it was the same dog that'd been with Flabberguts, white foam all around his mouth which kind of collected in the corners and hung down like two huge bogies. He was a bit of a scatty dog, laughing one minute and growling the next, but I didn't bother him and luckily, he didn't bother me.

I saw a police car in the distance. It was cruising slowly, as if the cops inside were looking for troublemakers. I wondered whether I should go and tell them what had happened to me. I wondered if they'd believe me. What if they decided I was a troublemaker? I decided not to say anything, just in case. They kept driving and left me and the dog and the other people who were in the park, though even most of them were leaving now.

It was almost dark. Stars had started showing themselves in the sky and I was getting pretty nervous.

A bat flew out of one tree and into another. Then I saw a second bat. "Hope they're not vampires," I said to the dog. As I watched them I realized there were stacks of them, maybe a hundred, or a thousand.

What if they attacked me? And bit me on the neck and drank my blood like they did in the movies? The dog started getting weird. He was scooting around on his bum like he had an itch or something. Or like he was trying to stop himself from pooing. I tried that once when I was little. It didn't work, though. I just ended up with poo halfway up my back. I sat on my foot another time, and that was even worse.

The whole thing was getting me spooked. I looked at my watch and for the first time wished it wasn't one that told the time, but a fake one that was really a walkie-talkie. I could see more and more stars in the sky when the bats got out of the way, so it was getting pretty late. I wished the police would come back. Getting busted for being a troublemaker had to be way better than this.

What if the crocodiles escaped from that crocodile farm where Ms Duncan said they kept the bad crocs from all over Australia? We'd passed it just before we got to Munchies. *So did they eat kids?* I wondered.

I didn't know what to do or where to go. My dad had never said how long it would take for them to find you once they realized you were lost. But surely it shouldn't have been taking this long.

I started to cry.

Not bawling or anything like that. I was just crying like when you hurt yourself but you're on your own and there's no point putting on a big act because there's no one around to see it. At least it gave me something to do.

I just put my head down on the table, covered my neck so the bats couldn't see it, and cried. And I kept on crying until something nudged me on the shoulder.

I screamed. The bats had finally come for me, but their beaks weren't as sharp as I would have thought.

I tucked my head into my arms and started screaming. I was hit again and then I could feel two claws on my shoulders, shaking me. It wasn't just the bats, it was the crocodiles as well. The dog set up barking and I thought he was going to start on me too.

I was being pushed and shaken and I could hear someone saying, "Hey, hey, hey, it's okay, it's okay."

I looked up, and it was one of the policemen from before.

"LOOK OUT!" I yelled at him. "The bats and the crocs are attacking!"

He kind of laughed and said, "It's okay, son. It's all right, the bats are fine. They eat berries; not boys. The crocs are all asleep at the crocodile farm. It's okay, everything's all right."

"Oh," I said, feeling a bit silly.

"What are you doing here?" he asked, sitting down next to me on the bench.

"I'm waiting for someone to find me," I sniffed, straightening up and wiping away the tears.

"It's a bit late for hide-and-seek, isn't it?"

"I'm not playing hide-and-seek," I said. Did he think I was stupid? "I'm waiting for my teachers to come back and find me. They left me here when we were all getting dinner and my dad said that when you're lost you should stay where you are so everyone knows where to find you."

"Your dad's right about that. Now what's your name, son?" he asked.

"Fergus," I said. "And we're going camping in Broome."

From there I told him the whole story of how the others had gone off without me.

We climbed into his car, which was more of a truck really. He got on the radio and started talking to someone or other, and even used the special code like they do on TV. He showed me how to turn on the siren and even let me push the button to make the lights work. His name was Marshal, and his badge said Sergeant.

Marshal took me to the police station and said again that everything was going to be okay. He said that a lot. He showed me a cell, but there weren't any prisoners, and he gave me a Coke, which I wasn't supposed to have. He was a nice cop, and I told him, and he said, "We're all nice!"

"Not the one that gave my mum a speeding ticket," I said. "Mum said he was lower than a snake's belly. She said that scumbag could kiss her big old butt and should go and solve a crime instead of raising revenue, whatever that means."

Sergeant Marshal kind of laughed. "She must be quite a lady, your mum."

"Yeah, she is," I said.

Marshal let me wait in the "lock-up", as he called it, for Ms Duncan to come and get me. He didn't lock it, though. He said it was bad luck, and that was the last thing I needed.

Ms Duncan apologized a lot when she arrived at the police station. She kept asking me if I was all right and if there was anything I wanted. I said I was fine, but she just kept muttering to herself about how sorry she was and, "Dear oh dear oh dear," and things like that. The whole way to the camp she kept apologizing and saying, "These things happen sometimes," and, "What an adventure that must have been!"

Yeah right! I thought. *Nearly being eaten alive by bats and crocs, cool!*

When we got to the camp, Mr Ford and Mr Roseman were up waiting for me. All the other kids were asleep in their tents. They asked me if I was all right as well and I said I was. They showed me my tent and I asked who set it up. They said Flabberguts Harvey had with Mr Ford. The ropes ran down to the pegs in the ground, not across to the trees. My dad wouldn't be happy.

I asked if they had cleared the ground properly and Mr Ford said that they had. There were no trenches around it, so he dug them for me right there and then, while Mr Roseman leaned against a tree, smoking and giving advice.

When they were sure everything was all right, they said I should go to bed.

I crawled into the tent and Flabberguts was asleep. I took my clothes off, put on my PJs and got into my sleeping bag. I could hear the teachers talking quietly. At least I wasn't alone anymore.

Then Flabberguts rolled over and farted.

Toolman

Maurice O'Toole, or Maurice *the* Tool as Paul Laughnan and I call him, has got to be the most spoilt boy in the whole world. Sometimes I think that's why we're friends – I get the spoils of his spoiling, if you know what I mean.

His dad works for one of the TV stations and goes overseas all the time. Whenever he comes home, he brings Maurice these amazing presents.

He was the first one in our class to have a Razor scooter, a Digimon and a digital TV. He was the first to have a DVD player. He's got everything. And he's got a mobile phone that vibrates and plays "Jingle Bells" when it rings, even when it's not Christmas.

As I said, Maurice and I are friends; it's just that his mum seems to think it might be better if we weren't. For some reason – and it has never been explained to me in a way that makes any sense – she reckons I'm a bad influence on him, or maybe we're a bad influence on each other.

"You two, you two, you two!" says his mum whenever we're together. "What is wrong with you two? Why can't you be good? What is it with being bad? What's the attraction? Especially you, Fergus, but both of you: what, what, what?"

"I don't know," one of us usually says. I mean, what's the question anyway? "I don't know," is the best thing to say when you're in trouble, and it covers most situations. Ignorance, despite what our parents always tell us, is often the best form of defence. That or crying. And when it comes to trouble, my mum's got nothing on Maurice's mum. She's mad. And not angry mad, but *loony* mad.

A while back, Maurice's dad bought him a Playstation in Japan. It was one of the new ones, a P2. His dad reckoned that if you knew how to make a missile, and you knew how to launch it, you'd be able to steer it into the enemy's headquarters with the P2 joystick, but you'd have to put a camera in the missile's nose so you could see where it was going. "That's how good the P2 is, you guys," his dad said to us.

"Cool," we said together.

"Can you get us a camera from the TV station to put into the nose of the missile, so we can watch it blow things up, Mr O'Toole?" I asked.

"Call me Tooley. And I tell you what, Fergus: after you make me a missile, I'll get you the camera. How does that sound?"

"Cool," we both said again. But we didn't have a clue how to make a missile. Instead, we played one of the games that Maurice had. It was awesome. You got to really belt each other and, given that I couldn't beat Maurice in a real fight, I was happy to whop him on the P2.

So that's what we used to do. After school, we would go to his house and belt the daylights out of each other on the computer.

On this particular day, Maurice's mum came into the lounge room and had one of her spac attacks, for no apparent reason at all. She just came into the room and started yelling about this or that and what a mess the house was, and his room was, and the lawn was, and the shed was, and her world was. Especially what a mess her world was. "How did I get here? Where am I going? Look what

101

I've become!" she was raving. She'd flipped right out.

"You two turn that wretched machine off and go outside and get some fresh air. You can mow the lawn and wash the car and clean out the fly wire room and anything else you can think of doing. I just do NOT want to see a child, ANY CHILD, again before dinner!"

"I've got to go home," I said. It didn't sound like much of an afternoon and Maurice the Tool's place wasn't that interesting to be around if I wasn't belting him on his video game.

"You will *not* go home, young man!" his mum bellowed. "You come around here every afternoon and wallop my son on that stupid game, so now you can help him give the chores a wallop as well."

"But, I..."

"No buts, no NOTHING!" she shrieked. She was obviously insane. "Mow that lawn and clean out that fly wire room with my son NOW! NOT YESTERDAY, NOT TOMORROW, NOW!!!!!!!!!!" The men from the loony bin would be carting her off any minute.

"But..."

"AAAAARRRRRGGGGGGGGHHHHHHH!!!" she screamed.

We ran outside.

"GET BACK IN HERE!" she roared as we got out there.

"But you said to get outside," said Maurice.

"Not until you pack away that ridiculous game. *Then* you can go outside."

So we did. We put away the Playstation 2 and ran outside before she could find something to throw at us.

We decided it would be easier to clean out the fly wire room than to mow the lawn, and as it turned out, that wasn't our best move.

The room she was yelling about was covered in fly wire, and the idea was to keep the flies out instead of letting them in. As I looked around the room, though, it was pretty obvious that the flies were stuck in there trying to get out, instead of battling to get inside.

Maurice got the fly spray and a broom. He also got some cotton thread, like the stuff Mum uses to sew up holes in Dad's socks. I didn't know what he was going to use it for, but I didn't have long to wait before I found out.

I picked up the fly spray and was getting

ready to wreak havoc when Maurice said, "Don't spray the flies yet. See if you can catch a big one first."

"Catch a fly? That's disgusting," I said. "Why would I want to go catching flies?"

"Ever eaten a fly?" he asked me.

"No, that's even more disgusting than catching them," I said.

"My dad says they're good for you, full of protein and stuff like that. He says if you ever get stuck in the desert you could live off them, and drink your wee for water."

"Has your dad ever been stuck in a desert?" I asked.

"I don't think so," said Maurice. "But he reckons that if the TV crew hadn't given the people on *Survivor* food and water, that's what they would have done. He made a documentary on it once. It was in black and white, so it must be true."

"It's still disgusting," I said again, and it really was.

"Well, it might be disgusting, but it could save your life. That's what my dad says anyway, and you know he's always right."

"To you maybe…" I muttered under my breath so he couldn't hear.

"Want to see some magic string?" he asked.

"Sure." I'd never even heard of magic string.

"You need to catch a fly."

"That's disgusting," I said again.

"You need a fly to make magic string," he said. So I scrounged around the fly wire room, eventually pinning a helpless insect in one of the corners. I took it over to him but he told me to hang onto it for a second. Then he made a loose knot in a length of the cotton, and inserted the fly's head in it. He tightened it around the fly's neck, but not so tight that he'd kill it.

Then he threw the fly in the air and off it flew, but with the cotton attached.

"Magic string!" he proclaimed. Then he grabbed the end of the string and flew the fly around like a kite. It was awesome. I couldn't wait to show Mum.

I found another fly and he helped me tie the cotton around its neck. Now we both had our own magic string, and we flew our flies all around the fly wire room. It was cool.

"Want to know how to get rid of it?" he asked me.

"Sure," I said. I would have thought you'd

just throw it away, but apparently not.

"You make the string loose, and then you rip it like this." He gave the fly some slack, then ripped the string tight and the fly was ripped in half. The head went one way and the body the other. No more fly!

We found that the bigger the fly, the better it worked, and they could last a bit longer as well.

This was almost as good as the time a while back that Dad and I fished for cane toads using Christmas beetles, in Queensland. It's much the same thing really: you tie a string to a Christmas beetle, and lay it out on the lawn. Eventually a dirty fat cane toad will come along and eat the beetle. When your line goes tight, it means you've caught a cane toad. You just wait till he swallows it and bring him in.

We caught stacks of them one Christmas. But it's not like fishing – you can't eat them – so we had to let them go. Dad reckons the best way to kill a cane toad is by sticking it in the freezer. "They just go to sleep and don't wake up," he said.

"What do you do with them when they're dead?" I asked.

"Stick them in the mulcher, grind them up, mix them up with soil, and use it as fertilizer."

"Why don't you just stick them straight in the blender when you catch them? That'd be much more fun; there'd be mess everywhere."

"Because, Fergus, that would be cruel, and one thing the Kipper family is not, is cruel. Do you understand?"

"I think so," I said. That didn't include being cruel to flies, though. No one likes flies; not even my dad.

Maurice and I played with the magic string for a while, and then he suggested we race our flies. "How do we do that?" I asked him.

"Pull their wings off and they run around because they can't fly," he said. I never realized some people thought there was so much fun you could have with a fly.

"Hey," I said. "I just thought of a joke. What do you call a fly without any wings?"

"I dunno," he said.

"A walk! Get it? They ca—"

"Yeah, funny one," he said, cutting me off, but he didn't laugh. *Maurice the Tool,* I thought.

Maurice's mum came out and said, "What on earth do you two think you're doing?

I thought I asked you to tidy the fly wire room?"

"We are," protested Maurice.

"Well, hurry up," she said over her shoulder as she huffed back into the house. Maurice's mum huffed a lot.

Maurice sprayed the fly spray everywhere. He got on a stool and sprayed the high corners, and on his knees to spray the low ones as well. He wouldn't let me do any of it, though, which was a bit annoying. It looked like much more fun than sweeping.

The poisoned flies were buzzing and bleating and slowly dying. I started sweeping them into a pile. There must have been millions of them. Occasionally one would try and escape in its final death throes, but it never got very far – I made sure of that.

I asked Maurice where the dustpan and brush were, but he said not to worry about that. He just grabbed the broom off me and swept them out the fly wire door and into the barbecue, which was a pit in the middle of the patio. "They'll add protein to the chops next time we have a barbie," he said, and who was I to argue with that? No way I'd be there, though.

I caught one of the flies that was still straggling and dared Maurice to eat it. He said, "No way, that's disgusting!"

"But your dad says they're good for you."

"Only if you get caught in the desert," he said.

"So pretend you're in the desert," I said. "Besides, I dared you."

"Darers go first!"

"Fine," I said. I picked up a fly and pretended to put it in my mouth, but I really kept it in my hand and made a lot of stupid faces pretending to swallow it. "Now you do it," I said. "Unless you're chicken."

"I'm not chicken," he said. "I'll do it. He picked up a fly and stuck it in his mouth.

"You didn't put it in your mouth!" I said.

He opened his mouth to show me it was there. It was disgusting. The fly tried to escape and he closed his mouth so it couldn't.

"Now you should drink some wee," I said. "Your dad reckons that's okay too. Go on, I dare you."

"Darers go first," he said again.

"No way, I'm not going to drink wee. You do it," I said.

"As if."

109

"Chicken."

"No, I'm not."

"Chicken," I said again.

"I know you are, I said you are, so what am I?"

"You're a gutless chicken," and I started making chicken noises at him.

"I am not a chicken," he said, and he came at me with arms flailing through the air. He was trying to hit me and kick me and pull my hair all at the same time. He was yelling, "I'm not a chicken, I'm not a chicken," and I was starting to think he was a bit loony like his mum.

She came storming out the door, and pulled Maurice the Tool off me.

"Are you two completely MAD? What's going on?" she asked.

"Nothi—" I started, but Maurice got in first.

"He's trying to make me drink wee. He says if I don't, I'm chicken."

"Why on earth would you want him to drink wee?" she asked me. She was really looking at me strangely, maybe even a bit cross-eyed. "WHAT'S WRONG WITH YOU? DO YOU DRINK WEE IN YOUR HOUSE?"

"No, but Maurice says that—"

"GET OUT OF THIS HOUSE!" she bellowed. "STAY AWAY FROM MY MAURICE! GO ON, GET, GET, GET…"

She was yelling at me like I was a dog. I ran out the back of the house and didn't look back. She was frightening. I thought she was going to tear me apart.

I waited a while before I went back to Maurice's to have a go with his Playstation. She didn't actually rip me to pieces, she kind of growled at me next time I saw her. But that was usual.

Dufus

"Grumpy old bugger," said Mum.

"I'll go to court, I'm happy to go to court, I have a lot of friends in court. You just let that stinky dog of yours off the lead one more time and I'll have a ranger down here tanning your hide and dragging you and your mangy mutt off to the pound so fast you won't feel your feet touch the ground." The old man seemed quite upset.

"Yeah, righto!" said Mum. "Whatever you reckon, old-timer." She didn't seem too happy either.

I stayed out of everybody's way, skimming stones across the swimming pool. I was trying to get them to bounce a couple of times on the surface before they leaped out the other side and into the Pacific Ocean. That was the best thing about ocean pools, but you could only do it at high tide; if you tried at low tide, the stones just skimmed straight into the wall.

"And tell that rodent child of yours to stop

throwing stones into the pool. The cleaners have got enough trouble dealing with the moss, so the last thing they need to worry about is getting a tractor in there to get all the stones out."

"Oh, don't be so ridiculous!" snorted my mother. "The ocean drops rocks in here every time there's a storm. God. Have you listened to how old you sound? Don't you remember what it was like when you were younger and old people told *you* what to do? Remember how old and stodgy they sounded? Well, that's how you sound now, you old fart!" I'd never heard Mum call anyone that before. Cool.

"Don't you go talking to me like that, you whipper-snapper! I'll have you in court for verbal assault before you can say 'Jiminy Cricket'. Besides, that young punk could hurt someone. Those rocks he's skimming can bounce off the surface and ricochet anywhere. I've seen eyes come out from less. What kind of a mother are you?"

"Stick it up your jumper, you relic," said Mum, as she wiped away some sea water that was leaking out of her nose. Then she covered one nostril and blew her nose into the air. "Tramp," she winked at me.

"That's lovely, that is. Perhaps you'll teach him to poo on the path like your dog does as well!"

I skimmed another stone. Mum looked at me and said, "Let's go." I called our dog, Dufus, who was peeing on the water fountain, put my t-shirt over my shoulder and started up the path.

"Have a terrific day, won't you!" Mum smiled at the old man.

"You too," he said. "And get a lead for that mutt."

"His name is Dufus," I said. "And he's not a mutt." Mum shushed me and gave me a hurry-up prod in the back.

We got Dufus a little while after Skozz died. I don't know whether Mum and Dad got him for us kids or for themselves. Dufus is twice the size Skozz was. He doesn't fit into Skozz's kennel, eats twice as much, and I tell you he can lay them the size of cucumbers. He must do it five times a day, because there's always dog poo all over the place: in the backyard, the front yard and up the side of the house.

It's the sneaky ones up the side that I hate the most. They're the easiest to step in because they're usually hidden by leaves from the filthy jacaranda tree that seems to relieve itself even more than the dog. And as if he doesn't do it enough at home, every time he goes for a walk he has a spray as well. I'm sure he poos more than he eats and, frankly, I can't figure out how. He's a good dog, but he's not Skozz. Not yet anyway.

"Stupid old bugger," Mum said at the old man again.

"Yeah, stupid old bugger," I said.

"Watch your language," she said to me.

"Sorry, Mum."

Dufus ran up ahead. He ran everywhere really. He only stopped to lay one, so he stopped a fair bit.

I was sick this day; that's why I hadn't gone to school. I wasn't really sick, but I just didn't feel like learning. I pretended I was to Mum, you know, holding my tummy and saying, "Oh, it hurts, it hurts," and groaning a lot.

She just said, "Okay, if you're sick you're sick, so go back to bed and we'll see how you feel at lunchtime."

I asked her to put the telly in my bedroom, but she said daytime telly would make me even sicker.

I jumped into Mum and Dad's bed anyway.

They had a telly in their room, so I changed the channel to the cartoons and settled in for the long haul. My sister, Elizabeth, came in and raided Dad's change box. "That's stealing," I said, "and you're not allowed to steal."

"You'd know," she said. I supposed she'd never let me forget about turning myself in for the attacks I had made on Dad's jangle box. "It's for the bridge toll. Dad told me to get it. What are you doing anyway? Why aren't you getting ready for school?"

"Because I'm sick," I said, "and Mum said I can stay home."

"Whatever," she said. Which she said about most things, unless it was Sistahs. She loved Sistahs. They were one of those girl bands, and they were sisters; there was Alice, Sally and Maddy Meagher, and the other one, Monique Rooney. They'd sung at my sister's school the year before, and she got all of their autographs and even a photo with Monique. She was my favourite, though there was no way I was going to tell Elizabeth that. In fact, I wasn't telling anyone.

Elizabeth also loved the Melbourne football team, but only because of Stephanie Ellis's big brother Chris. He'd moved all the way from Sydney to play for them and even Dad reckoned he was pretty good, which meant he must have been because Dad reckoned that anyone playing football had to have rocks in their head, especially when they could be playing rugby.

Dad said football was soft, and the fellas who played it were a pack of show-offs in baggy shorts and shin pads with no guts for the hard ball. He'd played second grade rugby for Manly and said that he could have played first grade if his knees had been stronger, and he blamed that on my grandma for not giving him enough milk when he was a baby. I didn't always know what my dad was talking about, but I did know that when he was talking about rugby he was always right. He reminded me of it all the time.

My sister pulled her fist out of Dad's change box, stuck the coins in her pocket and scowled at me as she left the room. I turned up the cartoon. It was *Transformers*, and always better loud.

Dad came in, flicked the telly off and sat next to me on the bed. "Your mum tells me you're sick."

"Yeah..." I groaned. "I feel funny in the tummy." He put his hand on my forehead and said, "You don't feel hot to me. Are you sure you're not trying to wag school?"

"Daaaaaad," I whined. "I'm sick. Mum said I'm sick too – so I must be."

"Good enough for me, then," he smiled. He rubbed my hair, patted my head and gave me a kiss on the forehead. "Be a good boy for your mum then, okay?"

I felt like barking. He was treating me like the dog again. "Okay, see ya, Dad," I said. He went into the bathroom, cleaned his teeth, got a fistful of coins from the jangle box, saying "For the bridge toll,' and flicked the switch so *Transformers* came back on. *Excellent,* I thought to myself, *that means Dad says I can watch telly.* "Have a good sickie," he said.

My brother came in and stuffed his fat paw into Dad's change too. "That's stealing," I said to him. At least I was consistent.

"Dah, you'd know," he said. "It's for the bridge toll. Dad told me to get it for him. What are you doing anyway? Why aren't you getting ready for school?"

"I'm sick. I'm not going to school," I said to him. "And Dad already got money out for the bridge, and so did Elizabeth, so you can't be getting it too. You're stealing, aren't you?"

"It's for tomorrow's toll. You're not sick anyway, so if you tell on me I'll tell on you."

"I *am* sick, and Mum and Dad said I could stay home, so you can tell all you want. I haven't done anything wrong."

"You won't tell on me, though, will you?" Clint asked me. He was named after Clint Eastwood, the movie star. His middle name was Harry, after *Dirty Harry*, my dad's favourite Clint Eastwood movie.

"I dunno. Do you feel lucky, punk?" I teased him. It was the famous line from *Dirty Harry*, and it always upset him.

"Shuddup, idiot!" he said, and stormed out of the room, stuffing the coins into his front pocket.

Dufus came in and jumped on the bed and we watched the cartoons until the guy with the big head came on. He was talking to some other guy about what it was like to be part of a family of television performers and the guy was mumbling something about it being tough to get a word in at family dinners. It looked like it was tough to get a word in with the guy with the big head. I switched it off and mooched out to look for breakfast.

Mum asked me how I was feeling and I mumbled, "A bit better."

She huffed and puffed for a while and said, "Really, Fergus."

As opposed to my brother, I have no idea how I got my name. I can't think of any movie stars called Fergus. In fact, I can't think of anyone at all called Fergus. I've never even found it on one of those number plates for your bedroom door. "It's unique," says Mum. "Like you." I looked it up on the Internet, and there it was: "Fergus – man of choice". I liked that a lot more than the other name Mum and Dad wanted to call me: "Flynn – descendant of the ruddy one".

"Look, Fergus," Mum said. "I know you're not sick, so let's just go and have a day together, shall we? Just the two of us. How about a swim at the pool? Go and get Dufus and we can head off to the pool and work out just what we're going to do with the rest of the day. Okay?"

"Okay!" I said. How cool was this? My mum was letting me wag school, and we were going swimming.

That's when we ended up with the "grumpy old bugger" at the pool.

Dufus hadn't really been that bad. For him, he'd actually been pretty good. He hadn't dug up any grass, hadn't gone in the water, hadn't even bothered anyone with his stick. All he'd done was dig in the corner of the beach under the rocks, where no one goes.

It wasn't much to us, but it must have been something to the old grouch.

He was walking up the hill in front of us. Huffing and puffing and grumping the whole way. "A good hot summer would fix him," said Mum, though I didn't really get what she meant.

The old man got to his car, threw his towel in, shut the door, locked it, and headed further up the hill towards the shops.

Mum and I kept walking up too, and we were doing a bit of huffing and puffing ourselves, but Dufus decided to stop and do that poo that the old man knew he would. We waited for him to finish, then Mum scooped it up into a plastic bag and we kept going. Mum crossed the street, which was a bit weird, because we were walking up the side our house was on.

She stopped at the old man's car, and started emptying the poo from the bag onto the ground in front of the driver's door. Dufus was a Rottweiler, and had a bit to give, so Mum scattered it everywhere.

Then she smiled at me. "Don't tell, okay," she said, "and I'll let you wag again."

"Cool," I said. And she did.

The Incident

Ding dong.
Ding dong, ding dong, ding dong.
Knock, knock, knock.
BANG! BANG! BANG!

I opened the door. Standing there, taking up the whole doorway, was Mrs O'Toole, Maurice's mum. Maurice, looking a bit sheepish, was standing behind her.

"Hey, Maurice. Hi, Mrs O'Toole," I said.

"Hey, Fergus," said Maurice.

"Do NOT talk to that boy," Mrs O'Toole barked at Maurice. "And don't you talk to him," she snarled at me. "Is your mother home?"

"I'll get her."

What am I, an idiot? I thought. As soon as I said it, I realized it would have been better to say she wasn't home. Mum was watching her favourite TV show, *Home and Away*. I told her there was someone at the door and she said to tell them to go away.

"It's Mrs O'Toole," I said. Duh! Sometimes I could be so stupid. Now she'd want to go and talk to her! Mum made a grunting kind of noise and put on her I-wasn't-watching-soaps smile before coming around into the hallway to meet Maurice's mum.

"Did you know that your son tried to get my son to drink his own urine?" she said. She made the word "urine" sound like "wine": *you-Rhine*.

"Pardon?" said Mum.

"He tried to get Maurice to drink his own urine. Does he drink his own urine in your house?" Mum kind of laughed, but Mrs O'Toole didn't. "I'm serious. He's a bad influence on Maurice and if these two keep mucking around together, they'll end up as a pair of no-goods, which is something I do NOT want for my son."

"I don't think it's quite that bad," Mum said to Mrs O'Toole. "They're just kids. I think we can forgive them a few indiscretions, can't we?"

"I hardly call forcing urine down poor Maurice's throat an 'indiscretion'. I think these two could afford to spend more time apart, making new friends, broadening their horizons. Being good! Okay?"

"I didn't force him—" I began, but Mum gave me the look, so I shut up.

"Bernice, I don't know exactly what happened, but whatever it was, it obviously wasn't good," said Mum. "How about we keep an eye on the boys, watch them, and just make sure they play by the rules? What about that?"

"I suppose so. But if there's anything else, if your son does anything like that again, they won't be able to see each other at all, ever! Do you understand that, Fergus?" she said, icing me with her bloodshot eyes.

"Yeah, all right, but—"

"All right." Mum interrupted me again with a forceful tug to my side. "And I'll be sure to sort this urine business out." This time she said "urine" the same way as Mrs O'Toole. Maurice and I waved at each other and our mums shook hands. We went inside.

I was waiting for Mum to blow up at me, but she went back to the lounge room and watched the end of the soap. She loved *Home and Away*, especially the weddings and the funerals. She said you could set your clock by them, they were so regular.

When it finished, she asked me what happened and I told her my version of the story. How Mr O'Toole, or Tooley, as Maurice's dad liked us to call him, had said you could drink it if you were dying of thirst in the desert, and I said to Maurice, "So pretend you're in the desert." I explained to her it was just a joke anyway. Mum told me to grow up and said that if I wanted to play with Maurice, we should do it at our house, or if I had to go to his house, I should only go when his mum wasn't home, just for a while anyway.

So that's what we did. But it was better going to his house because he had stacks more stuff. This time, Tooley brought home one of Luke Skywalker's old helmets. It was the one Luke used in the film *Star Wars* to fly his starship, and it was kind of smashed up. Luke apparently let Maurice's dad borrow his helmet when Tooley was flying in one of the starships (he was testing it out to see if the TV station he worked for wanted to buy it and use it as a corporate jet). After he got back, Luke said that he could keep the helmet, especially given that it was so smashed up and all.

Maurice said that his dad would have got

Darth Vader's helmet as well, but that Darth Vader needed it to breathe and he didn't have another one handy.

I asked Maurice to prove the helmet was real and he just said that his dad said it was real, so it was. "He makes TV shows, even documentaries; he doesn't need to lie. It's as simple as that," he said.

I told my dad about it and he sort of laughed and said next he'd try and tell me there was no Santa Claus. Then we both laughed because even Maurice the Tool wasn't *that* stupid.

In the end, Maurice and I came up with a plan that would prove whether the helmet was real or not. It was a perfect plan, and simple too, and I think it was Maurice's idea; not mine. That's what I told Mum and Dad after, anyway.

Maurice's mum had a dog called Flog. It was a stupid little white dog that used to sit on her lap whenever she picked us up from school. Flog was one of those dogs that didn't bark, but kind of miffed instead. He didn't go *bark bark,* or *arf arf*, but *miff miff miff!* And every time I got in the car, that little rodent of a dog miffed at me, and I hated it.

Like I said, our plan was simple. To test the helmet we decided to strap it onto Flog's head. As it turned out, we were able to fit the whole dog inside the helmet. We used the chin-strap to hold Flog in and put him on the driveway below Maurice's bedroom window.

Then Maurice and I ran upstairs and looked out to see if we could see Flog inside the helmet. Sure enough, there he was, directly below us. All we could see of Flog was his little tail sticking out the back of the helmet, but we could hear him *miffing* like crazy. He must have been on his feet and trying to escape because the helmet was moving, and started to run around by itself. From where we were, it looked like Luke Skywalker had a white ponytail and his head had been chopped off and it was rolling around on the O'Tooles' driveway. It looked cool.

If our plan was going to work, though, we needed to keep Flog and the helmet still.

Maurice sent me to the kitchen to get something for the dog to eat. All I could find were the dirty plates from lunch, so I stacked all the leftover sausages and tomato sauce onto one plate and took it outside for Flog.

We needed Flog to be in exactly the right

position for our test to work. Maurice got me to move him a bit this way, then a bit that way, then some more another way, until he was satisfied. Then I put the scraps in front of him and Flog started tucking in straight away. *Pretty good dog food,* I thought. *Pretty good Fergus food, too.* So I took half a sausage for myself.

When I got back upstairs, I found Maurice hanging out the window. All I could see was his fat backside wriggling around with his crack sticking out the top of his shorts. It wasn't pretty, and I only hoped he wouldn't fart.

I squeezed in next to him and sure enough, there was Luke Skywalker's helmet with Flog's tail still sticking out of it. He was getting stuck into the plate of leftover sausages and sauce, and the only thing that seemed to be worrying him was not getting the food into himself fast enough.

It was helmet testing time.

We decided that if the helmet was the real deal, not some tourist fake, then we'd be able to drop a brick on it from where we stood and it wouldn't smash. Not only would the helmet survive, but so would whatever was inside it.

In this case, Flog the dog.

These were fairly reasonable assumptions, and given we both wanted to see the brick hit Luke Skywalker's helmet, neither of us could actually be wearing it at the time of the test.

We would have used Maurice's little sister, she would have been perfect. She wasn't even one yet and couldn't walk or crawl or anything. She would've just lain there under the helmet and we could've dropped whatever we wanted on her.

Neither of us liked Maurice's sister. She cried *all* the time. Maurice reckoned it was amazing that a baby's head had that much water in it. He said she cried when she went to bed, when she woke up, when his mum put her in the car, when she took her out. Just all the time. It drove him mad, and it was a bit annoying for me too. In fact, we reasoned that if the helmet was a fake, it might at least have shut her up for five minutes. But she was out with Mrs O'Toole, so we used Flog instead. It was going to shut him up for a while too.

Maurice and I agreed that, at the end of the countdown, he should drop the brick on the helmet containing the dog. He got to drop the brick because it was his helmet. I tried to get him to do "scissors, paper, rock" for it, but he said, "If anyone is going to smash my helmet, it'll be me. Okay?" That seemed fair enough, though I did get to have a second brick in case he missed.

We ran it like a blast-off. He was the rocket commander and I was Mission Control. We did a systems check.

"Dog in position?"

"Check."

"Brick in position?"

"Check."

"Helmet in position?"

"Check."

"Dog in helmet?"

"Check."

"All systems go! Houston, begin launch."

"Ten, nine, eight, seven..."

"Houston, this is Mission Control, we have a problem," I announced.

Flog had moved, and exposed the plate. This meant that if we dropped the brick and missed the helmet, the plate would break. If there was one thing we definitely were not allowed to do, it was smash plates.

"Abort, abort, abort! Mission Control, this is Houston. We have aborted blast-off at this time..." said Maurice in his best American accent.

I belted down the stairs to reposition Flog and the plate. I checked with Maurice who said the dog in the helmet was in the right spot, and I raced back up the stairs to continue the countdown.

"Houston, this is Mission Control, the problem has been contained. We believe we are now in a position to launch. Copy that, Houston?"

"Mission Control, we copy. Thank you for your assistance. Ten seconds to blast-off and counting."

"Ten, nine, eight, seven..." The dog wasn't moving. "Six, five, four..."

"Clear from Mission Control, we are in go mode!"

"Three, two..."

"Clear from Houston..." I yelled.

"ONE..."

"BLAST-OFF!!!!!" we yelled together.

Maurice dropped the brick. It was as if it fell in slow motion.

At the same time the brick was falling, Maurice's mum and baby sister pulled into the driveway. We all watched as the brick sailed towards the helmet that was protecting the dog.

Mrs O'Toole screamed, the baby screamed, we screamed, but the greedy rodent didn't look up from the plate of scraps in front of him.

It was a perfect launch. The brick landed right on top of the helmet.

THWACK!!

"FLOOOOOOOOOOOOOGGGG!!!!!!!!!!!!!!!!!!" wailed Mrs O'Toole. But it was too late.

The helmet had split wide open, smashing Flog, and splashing blood and guts all over the place. It was a mess – a hideous, horrendous mess.

Then there was silence. I looked at Maurice and he looked at me. We both looked at Mrs O'Toole and then all of us looked down at Flog. It was terrible.

It was horrible.

The helmet was a fake.

The plate was broken.

Mrs O'Toole started screaming again, Maurice started crying, and I started thinking about getting home. The plate had smashed into a thousand pieces and Flog just lay there.

"You idiots, YOU IDIOTS! What were you doing? WHAT ON EARTH DID YOU THINK

YOU WERE DOING?" Maurice's mother was terribly upset. "You two get down here this instant, immediately, pronto, NOW!!!!!!"

We ran down the stairs. What had we done?

Even though neither of us really liked Flog, we certainly hadn't wanted to kill him. I was suddenly glad we hadn't used Maurice's sister after all. Then we would've been in *real* trouble.

We definitely hadn't wanted to smash the helmet, even if it was a fake.

By the time we got downstairs, Mrs O'Toole had managed to separate Flog from the broken plastic. It was hard to know where to look. Tears were streaming down her face and the little dog was cradled in her arms, covered in blood and looking as dead as a footy without its bladder.

I almost felt sorry for it.

"It's YOU!" she yelled at me. "Always you, you, YOU! It's not enough for you to try and poison my son, is it? Now you kill my dog! Why don't you take my daughter as well? You're evil. EVIL!"

I started backing off. No one had ever called me *evil* before. I think she even shocked herself. Everyone went silent, not knowing what to say or where to look.

And then we heard it: very quiet, but quite distinctive.

Miff.

Then a little louder. *Miff miff…*

It was Flog the dog *miffing* at me, like he did whenever I was in their car. "He's alive!" squealed Maurice. "We didn't kill him! He's alive, he's alive!" He was laughing. "It's okay, Mum, we didn't kill Flog." And with that he began picking up the pieces of his helmet, trying to fit them back together.

Mrs O'Toole showed no regard for the blood that was all over Flog, and kissed him all over the face, cooing, "Floggyfloggyfloggy-floggyfloggy…" It was sickening.

Then she stopped and said that it wasn't blood all over Flog, but tomato sauce. She looked furious again and I thought her head was going to blow off her shoulders.

"He's covered in sauce. Why is my dog covered in tomato sauce? What ELSE have you two sickoes been doing to my dog?"

"We just put sau—" started Maurice, but she was onto him in a flash.

"Get inside. GET INSIDE!" she screamed.

He was bawling. I turned to go as well.

"What did I say to you, Fergus? What did I say to your mother? I said STAY AWAY FROM MY SON! is what I said. Isn't it? Isn't that what I said? Now you can stay away from my dog too. And you'd better stay away from my daughter as well! What's wrong with you anyway? Are you simple, or is it the devil that's got you? Get out of here. And I never, ever, EVER want to see you near my son or my dog again. EVER!!!!!!!!"

I ran away before she had a chance to see the tears streaming down my face.

Maurice told his mum and dad the whole thing had been my idea, and that it was me who dropped the brick on Flog, not him. His mum rang my mum and they talked on the phone for ages. Mum even missed *Home and Away* because of it. She missed the sound, anyway; I think she kept it down so Mrs O'Toole couldn't hear it. When she got off the phone she said, "I'm not talking to you about this now. I want to discuss it with your father. Then we'll talk about it. All of us. Maybe even in the study."

But that didn't happen, so maybe it wasn't so bad after all.

They sat me down at the kitchen table and said to tell them what had happened. What had *really* happened, and not some story to stop me getting into trouble. They told me for the hundredth time that lying was stupid and if I did it I'd get caught, so I told them the truth. I told them how the whole thing had really been Maurice's idea, how I'd thought it was dangerous and we shouldn't have done it at all. I told them how I thought it shouldn't have made a difference whether the helmet was real or fake; it was a present and that was all that mattered. I told them everything they wanted to hear. And I think they liked it.

I got sent to bed, but I still got to have pudding.

Flog the dog ended up being okay, but only just. The brick crashing through the helmet had broken all of his legs and his tail. So for the next four weeks he had just about everything in plaster and had to be taken for a walk on Maurice's skateboard.

I saw him once when Mrs O'Toole came to pick up Maurice from school. He was *miff miffing* like crazy and looked like a noisy toy dog with four wooden legs and a spare one sticking out of his backside.

Stupid dog.

Mum said that Mrs O'Toole would settle down eventually. She said I should probably wait for the dog's legs to heal before I rushed over to play with him again. But that was fine anyway. By then his sister might finally have stopped crying.

Uncle Dad

I had the most amazing dream last night. I went fishing with my uncle, only he wasn't my uncle because I kept calling him "Dad". So he was my Uncle Dad, which was kind of strange.

The sky was a brilliant purple, the sea was blue and everything was sort of blurry around the edges. We were on Uncle Dad's boat, a speedboat that went really fast but never got bumpy, which is nothing like my real uncle's boat. It's old and slow and it stinks. That's why he calls it a stinkboat, I suppose.

I didn't think I'd ever get sick in this boat, but I have in my uncle's. It was shocking. I thought I was going to die. It felt like I'd spew up everything I'd ever eaten, and a whole lot of things I hadn't. But not in this boat; not that day. It didn't feel like that at all.

Uncle Dad gave me his fishing glasses to try on. They were awesome. The sky turned blue, the blurry edges were gone and the sea became yellow. I could see fish in the sea, stacks of them. I told him about the fish, but he said there weren't any fish here. He couldn't see them anyway. He said he couldn't see diddly without his glasses, so I gave them back.

When I took the glasses off I couldn't see the fish anymore. The water went back to its old colour and once again the world had a bit of a soft edge. I told my uncle that without his glasses I couldn't see anything.

"Maybe you should dream yourself a pair," he said. So I did, and it was cool.

There were fish everywhere. They were big and small, light and dark, fat and skinny. It was kind of like looking at people. Each one sort of the same, but just a little different. It was like being in Brunswick Street. They've got all sorts down there.

My dad is a really good fisherman. My uncle's good, but not as good as Dad. They both reckon I'm a bloody good fisherman. Whenever I'm with them I always catch fish, always. They reckon I'm a freak: a good one, though.

Uncle Dad put some bait on my hook and let me cast it in myself. The cast was a beauty too. It flew through the air and landed with a gentle *plonk*. A circle of waves came from where it landed. They grew bigger and bigger and I could see yellowtail surfing them as they broke before the boat. It would have been cool to have some kind of mini, remote-controlled surfer. I thought about that every time I went to the beach and saw the waves that were too small for me but would have been perfect for Big Jim or Action Man or someone like that.

I watched my bait sink and, as it did, a little poddy mullet watched it as well. He sniffed and wondered if it was worth a taste. It was, and the little mullet opened its mouth wide and swallowed it whole.

I don't think the mullet expected to find my hook in his mouth, and he fought and struggled as he tried to swim away.

"I'm on!" I yelped to Uncle Dad as the mullet struggled harder. We always said that when we hooked a fish.

"Bring him in," he said, "and remember, if he wants to run, let him run." He always said that. Even though fish can't run, he always said it.

I was reeling the mullet in when I saw a

squid following him. He was watching him, thinking about him, wondering if he was worth a squirt of ink. Apparently he was.

Suddenly the mullet disappeared in a cloud of black ink. I couldn't see through the cloud and I was wondering what was happening. The next thing I knew was the squid came out of the ink, and the mullet was nowhere to be seen. The squid now had the hook in *his* mouth, which meant that he must have eaten the poor little fish. *Poor mullet,* I thought. *What a way to go, being sucked into the mouth of a squid. Yuk!*

"Good stuff!" said Uncle Dad.

The squid was a bit bigger than the mullet, and he pulled a bit harder. Uncle Dad told me to be patient, tire him out, and we'd have the squid for lunch. "Just remember," he cautioned, "if he wants to run, let him run."

But the squid wasn't really big enough to run, if squid *can* run at all. I bet he wished he could have, though, because with all of his pulling and ink-squirting, he'd attracted the attention of someone else. There was a tailor watching that squid. Watching, thinking about him, wondering if he was worth a bite. And he was.

I reeled my line in as fast as I could to try and save the squid. But the tailor was too fast. This time in self-defence, the squid squirted another cloud of ink, and I couldn't see a thing. The sea was black. Then my line started pulling twice as hard as before, and from the ink came the tailor, and from the tailor's mouth came my fishing line. "YES, SIR!" I said to Uncle Dad. "I *am* a bloody good fisherman!"

I couldn't believe it, from a mullet to a squid to a tailor, and all on the one piece of bait.

I started reeling in the tailor as fast as I could. But the faster I wound, the further he swam away. If I stopped winding, he stopped running. So I did, and he did. It was a stale-mate. He looked at me and I looked at him; I looked at him and then he looked away and started running.

"Go, you good thing," said my uncle as the tailor took off. "He looks like he wants to have a run, so…"

"He's faster than Cathy Freeman," I said.

"Sure, I guess," he said. "Just keep the line taut; not tight, but taut."

"Okay, but what's taut?"

"Well, it's not tight and it's not sloppy. It's taut. Got it?"

"Kind of," I said.

"Just do what you're doing," Uncle Dad said as he watched the tailor bolt. And he did too. He would have kept going for miles, I reckon, if he hadn't run right smack bang into the mouth of a massive kingfish.

Ouch! That would have hurt.

I couldn't believe it. I took my fishing glasses off to see if it was really happening, but without them I couldn't see a thing. When I put them back on, the tailor was gone, and a kingfish the size of my uncle's leg was on the end of my fishing line.

Amazing. How good was this? It was like a fishing dream come true. It *was* a fishing dream come true.

My uncle got revved up when he saw the kingfish with my line in his mouth. "He's gonna run, Fergus," he said to me, sounding a bit excited. "He might run for us; he might run against us. If it's for us, keep it taut and wind your line like buggery."

"What?"

"Sorry. As fast as you can. If he runs away from us, just let him go and hang on."

Okay, fish can't really run, but no one had told the kingfish. He leaped out of the water like a scalded cat, then he took off for the depths of the Pacific Ocean. I was hardly strong enough to hold him, but I did, and just watched him go. And, boy, did he! I reckon he was more freight train than fish.

That kingy would have run all day; he was certainly strong enough. But there was something watching the kingfish that was just a bit stronger, a bit faster, and a whole lot hungrier.

It came up from the deep. I sensed it before I actually saw it. Uncle Dad went quiet and I think he knew what was coming too. Even the kingfish did; he was swimming for all he was worth. But instead of away from us, he was swimming *towards* us. Straight for the boat. He was attacking.

My line went slack and Uncle Dad started screaming, "Wind, wind, wind! Now's the time to give it buggery!" And I did, I wound like a madman. If I'd been beating eggs, there would have been froth all over the place. I still wasn't as fast as the kingfish, though, who was nowhere near as fast as the shark that was chasing him.

"NOAH'S ARK!!! It's a Noah's bloody ARK!!!" roared Uncle Dad.

"It's a SHARK, Uncle Dad! It's being chased by a SHARK!!!" I yelled back at him.

"THAT'S WHAT I JUST SAID! Now shuddup and get that kingfish in the boat before the shark gets him."

Stuff the kingfish, I thought. *What about us?* I was going as fast as I could, but I could tell we were in trouble. The shark would have us for mains once he'd demolished the kingfish, and if I was going to die, I was hoping it wouldn't be by having my body ripped apart in the mouth of a shark. I started thinking it might be a good time for my alarm to go off; even school would be better than this.

The shark thrashed his mighty tail, opened his massive jaws and was about to chomp down on the king, when the kingfish leaped in the air and soared over the boat. Hurdling it. The shark tried to follow, but he was too big to get out of the water. His tail was kicking like crazy and his choppers were going berserk, the rows of teeth shining like mirrors.

"AAAAAARRRRGGGHHHHHHHHHHH!!!"

The shark went *whump!* straight into the side of the boat.

I was screaming, Uncle Dad was screaming,

the shark was screaming, and the kingfish, he was gone. He'd spat the hook out of his mouth and disappeared. No goodbye, no thanks for saving him, nothing.

The shark had bitten a huge hole in the side of the boat. Water came pouring in. I was drenched, Uncle Dad was drenched and the shark kept flapping and flailing and thrashing around trying to get his lunch, which was me.

"WAKE UP, WAKE UP, WAKE UP!" I yelled to myself, hoping it was a dream. I didn't want to fish anymore, I didn't want to wear fishing glasses and I didn't want to be lunch for any big old shark. I was so scared and cold and wet, I just wanted to wake up.

"WAAAAAAAAKE UUUUUUUUUUUP!!!!!!" I yelled again.

The shark disappeared, the boat, Uncle Dad, everything. I was in my bed, with my spotty wallpaper and Demons duvet cover. I was still a bit scared, a bit cold – and very wet.

In all the excitement, the bed was wet.

Maybe because I'd been frightened, or maybe because of the water in the boat. (Touching water when you're asleep always

155

makes you pee.) Or maybe because the fishing glasses made the water too clear, or the kingfish startled me.

Or maybe I'd sucked too much water off my toothbrush after I'd cleaned my teeth, or maybe I should have gone to the toilet before I went to bed.

It could have been anything. Anything at all. I remembered Mum. What would I tell her? Maybe I should've just got the sheets off the bed and into the wash and said I thought it was sheets day. Nah, why would I have started doing it then, when she'd been at me for ages to do it before?

What could have made me wet my bed? I'd have to tell Mum, I'd just have to. It wasn't as if I could hide it; the sheets were saturated. She'd know for sure.

But what would I tell her? What excuse could I give her for wetting the bed at my age?

I suddenly knew I was going to tell her the truth.

I'd tell Mum that the shark made me do it.

Humpy Eggs

I should never have done it. No, I should have; I just should never have been caught.

It didn't seem like that big a deal anyway. When you've done as much planning as we had, it would have been a shame not to go through with it. That's the thing about planning, right? You plan for your mission to succeed.

And we kind of did.

We all wore black clothes, or as dark as we had anyway, and some bright spark thought up the brilliant idea of painting our faces black so we couldn't be seen in the dark. I'd seen in the movies where they took some coal from the fire and wiped it on their faces. The trick was to use cold coal; that way you didn't get burnt.

So there we were, me, Johnno and Joffa, our faces blackened and our clothes dark. Had it been night we would have been practically invisible. We even painted the egg box black, and the eggs inside black, so no one would see them either.

It had all been planned perfectly. It was just that I hadn't planned for the mission to end in my father's study.

I had been in the study before as part of a game of Truth or Dare. It was my tenth birthday and I was dared to kiss Missy Bait. I didn't want to, but a dare is a dare, and it was kiss her or tell the truth. That's how Truth or Dare works. You choose to do a dare, and that can be anything, or you can choose to tell the truth about something that the others ask. And they could have asked me anything, such as, "Do you like Missy Bait?" and I would have had to tell the truth. That would have been worse than kissing her, of course, because then everyone, including Missy, would have known that I did like her.

And for her to know that would have been the worst of all!

This way I got to kiss her without her knowing I liked her.

So I did it. I kissed her fair on the mouth like they do in the movies and it was sloppy and wet and disgusting and I loved it. I think she liked it too. But I didn't tell her that I did.

She asked me if I wanted to do it again. I said to her, "If you dare me, I will." And she did. So I kissed her again. It was just as disgusting and sloppy and wet as the first time and I liked it even more.

My dad came into the study when I kissed her the third time. He just barged straight in without knocking or anything. Straight in.

I nearly died, so did Missy, but it's not as if we were hugging or anything. It was just kissing. At first I didn't know whether Dad knew what we were doing. And it seemed I was right.

He said, "What are you two doing?"

"Nothing," I said.

"Were you kissing?" he asked.

I could see Missy turning a lovely shade of red. "Daaaaaaaaaaaaaaaaaaaaaad," I squealed. "We were not."

"Are you sure?" he asked, smirking.

I could feel my cheeks getting hot. I was sweating in my armpits and my eyes were burning as tears threatened. *Please don't let me cry,* I said to myself. I would rather have died than cry in front of Missy Bait. "Yes, Dad, of course I'm sure," I managed.

"It looks to me like you might have been kissing," he teased.

161

"Well, we weren't, were we, Missy?" She got up and ran out of Dad's study. I'm sure she was crying, and I wasn't far behind her.

"We weren't kissing, Dad."

He came over to me, sat on the couch and started tickling me in the ribs. "Have I got a kissy boy on my hands?" he cackled. "Hey? Have I got a kissy boy on my hands?" His fingers were digging into my ribs and I was squirming, trying to get away. "Mmmmmm? Is it a kissy boy I have before me? Huh? Hey? Kiss, kiss, kiss?"

"Stop it, Dad," I pleaded. "We weren't; I wasn't. You haven't got a kissy boy."

"I think I have, kiss kiss kiss. C'mon, give us a kiss."

"Stop it, Dad," I pleaded. The tickling was hurting. He was digging his fat fingers into my bony ribs and it made them sore instead of making me laugh.

"C'mon, loverboy," he squealed. "Give us a great big kiss."

I hated it when he got like this. He thought he was being funny, but he'd embarrassed me in front of Missy, and the tickling hurt. The more he laughed, the more it hurt, and I couldn't get him to stop. He must have thought my screams of protest were screams of joy. I started crying but I put my head down so he couldn't see my tears. I was so angry that I started to punch him to try and get him to stop.

"Hey, c'mon now. Hey, that's enough. Cut it out," he laughed. The tickling wasn't funny, and he wasn't funny, and now I couldn't stop crying. Crying so much I could hardly breathe. "It's okay," he said. "I was just teasing. I don't care if you were kissing. It's good if you were. I love kissing. I mean, I loooooooove kissing." He smiled as he started tickling me again.

"Stop it, Dad. Stop it!" I managed between sobs. "We weren't kissing. I don't even like her. I don't even like girls; they stink and they've got germs and you need needles if you touch them."

"Not your mother," said my father.

"She's not a girl."

"She used to be."

"Well, now she's Mum, so it doesn't matter anyway."

"It's really okay if you were kissing, you know," he said. He was being serious now.

"But I wasn't," I said.

"But it's fine if you were. I just want you to know that, okay?"

"Okay!" I said. He was getting annoying.

"Why don't you go back to your party now?" he said, as he wiped my face with his sleeve.

"Can you tell I've been crying?" I asked.

"No, matey. You just look like you've been kissing a girl," he squealed, and started up on the tickling again.

I laughed this time, and got free of him with a super karate chop to the shoulder, followed by a nose clamp and eyebrow rip, just like he'd taught me.

"Nice move, birthday boy! Have a good party," he said, smoothing down my clothes and fluffing my hair. "You're a big fella now. Why don't you come and give us a big kiss before you think you're too old to do it?" I did, and that was that. That was the last time I'd been in his study.

I wished I was in there for kissing a girl now. I was in more trouble this time than a fish out of water, or as Dad would say, "more crap than a Werribee duck".

I shouldn't have been there at all. That is, we shouldn't have been caught. If we'd all stuck to the plan it would have been all right, but we hadn't and it wasn't, and now I was sitting on Dad's lumpy chair, waiting for him to speak. It was always worst when he said nothing. That meant he was thinking about what he would eventually say.

We had set off from the house, our blackened faces almost as dark as our clothes, and we were heading for the Humpys. In our street, they were the family that nobody liked. Every street's got a family like that.

In our old street it had been the Gobbles, or the Turkeys as we called them. They were exactly like the Humpys: they never mowed their lawn. "Dirty dog breeders," Dad used to say. "All those bloody dogs drive me barking mad." I never knew why, they lived right up the other end of the street anyway. He reckoned illegally breeding dogs in a residential area was a disgrace. He said it brought the neighbourhood into disrepute. I'm not sure what that meant, but I'm guessing it wasn't good.

The Humpys didn't wash their cars, and their dogs pooed on everyone else's lawn, probably because the grass was so high on their own they didn't like it sticking into their bums. The Humpys didn't sweep their drive and they always had their blinds down. "They must be hiding something," my dad used to say. We used to take it upon ourselves to find out what it was, but it was pretty hard to see inside windows when the blinds were drawn.

So they were our targets on this secret mission. The plan was to egg their house, and we got there just as it was getting dark.

The lawn was still knee high and the blinds were drawn. It looked as if no one was home, except that the light was on at the front door.

We hid under the trees. The three of us had two eggs each, and we waited until there were no cars around so the order to fire could be given.

When we were almost ready, the Humpys' dogs started yapping inside. I said we should all go home before Mr Humpy came out and caught us, but the others called me a chicken, so I didn't say too much after that.

No one likes being called *chicken*.

When it was all clear, Joffa gave the order to "let loose with the egg bombs". He was our leader. Joff was older than me and Johnno, but only by a year. I was taller than him, but because he was the oldest he got to give the orders.

He was first to throw. His egg sailed in a high arc. It landed just short of the house, in the grass. He said it slipped from his hand.

I went as close to their fence as I dared and let rip with the biggest throw I could muster. But I must have hung on to the egg too tightly, because as I let it go, it squished in my hand and the shell only made it as far as the Humpys' fence. There was egg all over me and my arm and the other guys laughed their heads off.

"It was already broken," I squealed at them, but they kept on laughing.

"Yeah, right!" said Joffa. "You're a chicken and you can't throw an egg. I bet you could lay one though. *Ba hahahahahahahaha!*"

"I'm not chicken!" I said. "And I can throw an egg, you watch." My eyes were beginning to sting and I could feel my chin wobble. Sometimes I didn't like him.

Johnno threw his into the fence too, but it didn't break in his hand. I laughed at him and tried to get Joff to as well, but he just said, "Good one, chicken." And I hoped the new nickname wouldn't stick.

None of us had hit the house with our first egg.

I jumped the Humpys' fence so I could get closer in. There was no way I was having them call me a chicken again, so this time I would make sure I didn't miss. I hid behind a tree halfway between the house and the fence.

Joffa said, "I'm going for the front door." He let fly with the biggest throw I'd seen since Pop took me to the MCG to see the cricket. I watched as it sailed right for the front wall. Huge; it was like it was in slow motion. That egg just kept going and going and then BANG!!! It landed on the path next to the house.

The dogs inside, Hedgehog and Liz, went bananas. They were yapping like crazy.

Then Johnno and Joffa took off. Joffa scrambled up a tree and Johnno squeezed himself under a hedge. I was stuck. If someone had come out of the house, they'd have seen me running, so I had to hide where I was. I was petrified.

We expected Mr Humpy to come out at any minute. He must have heard the bang. It was huge.

The dogs were still going mad. Hedgehog was a stupid little dog, more of a rodent really. He was one of those Benji dogs, but not cute like the movie star. Liz was one of those Daewoo dogs, a boy dog with a girl's name because they'd lost another dog called Liz and tried to trick Denny Humpy by buying another dog before she came home from a school camp. But they couldn't get a girl. At least they got the breed right.

When Joffa's egg landed next to the house nothing happened. The dogs settled down and it was pretty obvious that the Humpys weren't home. They always left the dogs inside when they were out – another reason Dad reckoned they were strange.

Johnno and Joffa came back to the fence. I slid out from behind the tree and decided that since no one was home, I'd have a ping at the front door from where I stood.

I placed my index finger on the point of the egg and held my thumb on the round end. Mr Stainer, our science teacher, had told us it was impossible to break an egg by pushing from top to bottom and I was hoping he was right. For once, something they taught us in science was useful.

I pulled my throwing arm way back behind my head and took aim at the middle of the front door and closed one eye to make sure I got it perfectly.

One, I said to myself, and pulled my throwing arm back even further. *Two,* and the dogs started yapping again but I wasn't too worried about that. *THREE!* I roared as I threw the egg at the Humpys' front door.

What a throw! High and long and straight.

As the egg sailed through the air, though, the front door started to open. Slowly at first, and then with a great rush.

The egg was on its way, headed right for where the middle of the door had been and right where Mr Humpy was now standing, looking about his yard with a great big frown on his big fat face.

He was only wearing a pair of football shorts hanging halfway down his bum and he had an ice-cream in his big fat paw.

The egg was on target.

"LOOK OOOUUUTTT!!!!!!!!!" I yelled. I was frozen to the spot. Couldn't move. All I could do was watch.

Mr Humpy flashed a look at me and

started to say something, but he didn't have time and he didn't have a chance to duck. The egg was on him before he knew it.

SMACK! Right in the middle of his chest.

He dropped his ice-cream and clutched at his chest as shell and yolk dripped everywhere. "I'VE BEEN SHOT!" he roared. "HELP! HELP ME, SOMEBODY, I'VE BEEN SHOT!"

"YOU'VE BEEN EGGED!" yelled Joffa and ran away. Johnno was running too, faster than I think I've ever seen him. *Best I run too,* I thought, so I did, and headed for the fence as fast as my feet would carry me.

I could hear Mr Humpy behind me. "You kids come back here! YOU BLOODY KIDS COME BACK HERE RIGHT NOW!!!!!!!!!!" he was screaming. "NOW, NOW, NOW!!! I KNOW WHO YOU ARE, JOHNSON. MICHAEL BLOODY JOHNSON, YOU COME BACK HERE NOW!!!"

I turned around to look and he was running as fast as a fat old angry man could run, which was surprisingly fast.

I practically hurdled the fence; couldn't see Johnno and Joffa anywhere. They were long gone. I would've done anything to be chicken right then. I wished I wasn't there at all.

I kept on running till I was well away from the Humpys' house and then ran even further. I had no idea where old Humpy was, but I was just relieved to see that he wasn't behind me.

I was puffing so hard I could hardly breathe. All I could think of was the egg flying through the air and smashing in the middle of Humpy's chest. What a shot! Great throw!

"*Pssssst. Pssssst.*" I heard from underneath a bush.

I let out a little whistle. It was the secret code of all the guys.

A whistle came back, and I sent back a *pssssst pssssst*. It was Johnno. I was safe.

"Where's Joffa?" I puffed.

"He's gone home, you idiot," said Johnno. "He thinks it was me. He said *my* name."

"What?" I said. I hadn't heard anything, I'd been too busy running.

"Humpy, old man Humpy. It was my name he said! He yelled, 'Michael bloody Johnson, you come back here now!' He thinks it was me, and it was you. You'll have to go back and tell him it was you, because it wasn't me."

"How would he know it was you? We've got our faces blacked out. No one would know who it was. We'll be right." I could hear myself saying it, but I wasn't so sure.

"We better be, or you'll have to say that you did it, because if you don't I'll say you did, and you know I will."

He would've too. He'd told on me for nicking twenty cents off the floor of his mum's car, and this was much worse than that.

We decided to go home; Johnno was staying at my house anyway. Before we got there we washed the coal off our faces using the tap in someone's front yard. Johnno was still pretty angry about Mr Humpy thinking it was him, but by the time we were home we couldn't stop laughing.

And it *was* pretty funny. Mr Humpy standing there in his footy shorts chomping on an ice-cream and then – WHAM! – egg all over his chest and him wailing, "Help me, help me, I've been shot." The more we talked about it, the funnier it got. I could hardly breathe I was laughing so hard. By the time we got home we were just laughing at everything, even stuff that wasn't funny.

I nearly wet my pants laughing when we got to my house and saw Johnno's mum's car in the driveway. "The egg man's probably told on us," I laughed. Johnno laughed at this too, but then stopped.

"Do ya reckon?" he asked.

"Hardly," I said. I was sure it was okay, though, because his mum was always at our house, or my mum was at theirs. We laughed about that too.

We went into the kitchen to get a drink. Throwing eggs was a thirsty business. There were no parents anywhere, but from the kitchen we could hear them talking in the study. So we stayed in the kitchen.

The study door opened, and out came Dad, Johnno's dad – and Mr Humpy! I felt a sudden urge to go to the toilet. Johnno and I looked at each other and then at the kitchen floor. I don't think I'd ever found it so interesting.

Johnno's dad said to him, "You, in the car, now!" He sounded angry.

"But I didn't do anything. He threw it, not me." *Thanks pal*, I thought.

"I don't care, get in the car," he insisted.

"But Dad, I didn't DO anything!"

"NOW!" he said, grabbing Johnno's arm. He dragged him out the front door and left me, my dad and Mr Humpy in the kitchen.

Mr Humpy was still in his footy shorts with congealed egg dripping from his breasts.

"Go to the study," Dad said quietly. I hated it when he spoke like that: it meant trouble wasn't far away. I walked down the hallway where Mum was tut-tutting and shaking her head. She even sucked her teeth as I went past her. She wasn't going to save me. I sat in the study and started examining the floor in earnest.

I could hear Dad saying goodbye to Mr Humpy. "I really am sorry about this, Nigel," he said.

Nigel? What kind of name was Nigel? It sounded like a snitch's name.

"Yes," said Nigel. "I just thought it better we nip it in the bud before it got out of hand, mmmmm?"

"No worries, Nige," said Dad.

"Nigel," said Mr Humpy.

"Sorry. Right, Nigel it is. No worries, Nigel."

"Don't forget to send us the dry-cleaning bill for those football shorts either, Nigel," said my mum from the kitchen door.

"I won't," he said. And with that Nigel Humpy was gone.

And there I was, waiting in Dad's study.

I could hear Mum and Dad talking. Quietly. I thought I heard Dad laugh, but when he came in and shut the door behind him, he didn't look like he'd been laughing. Or even smiling. I went back to the floor.

"That was pretty stupid, wasn't it?" he said.

"We didn't do anything," I said, still not looking at him.

"Mr Humpy seems to think you did."

"It must have been some other kids," I said, looking at him for the first time. He wasn't impressed.

"So, let me get this straight because I think I'm a little slow. It was some other kids dressed in dark clothing who look like you and happened to be out tonight and who got home at the same time as you, who went to the Humpys' house?"

"Yeah, I suppose so," I said, hopeful that I was onto a winner.

"Who threw it?"

"I don't know."

"Who threw it?" he asked again.

"I don't know."

"It could have killed him."

"It was only an egg," I said.

"How do you know it was an egg?"

"What do you mean?" My chin was going on me again.

"How did you know it was an egg that could have killed Mr Humpy?"

"I *don't* know."

"You just said it was an egg."

"I was guessing."

"Who threw the egg?" he asked again. "Mr Humpy seems to think it was Johnno. But Johnno seems to think it was you. Was it?"

I thought about saying it was Joffa, but opted for the floor.

"I'm trying to be civil about this, son. Was it you? Did you throw the egg at Mr Humpy?" He was giving me every chance to lie, and every chance to tell the truth. The real question was, which would get me into more trouble?

"Five, four…" Oh no, the countdown. Three seconds to decide. My chin was having a fit and the tears were starting too. "Three, two…"

"*I threw it!*" I bawled as tears started falling down my face.

"Why?" he asked me. But it wasn't a quick "Why?", it was a long drawn-out "*Whhhhh-yyyyyyy?*"

"I don't know," I sniffed.

"Yes you do. You know exactly why you did it, *and* you know you shouldn't have. Jeeeeesus, I don't know what gets into you sometimes." Here was the lecture about what I should and shouldn't do. The trouble. Here at last was the trouble. And it looked bad; Jesus was getting involved, and when Jesus was involved, it was always bad.

Just agree, I said to myself. *Agree with everything and the trouble will be over faster.* "I know," I agreed.

"You know what gets into you, or you know why you shouldn't have done it, or you know why you did it? What? What do you know?" He was smarter than me.

"I don't know," I said. And I didn't.

"You're pathetic, you know that? You'd be better off to just tell the truth and face your punishment like a man. If you want to be treated like a grown-up maybe it's time you started acting like one. I'm disappointed in you. *Very* disappointed. I don't know, you're as bad as your brother. It's as bad as the time he stuck potatoes up Humpy's exhaust pipe and blew up his silencer. You're embarrassing. Go and put your football shorts on."

That was it? I thought. *That was the trouble?*

Now we're going to play football. Ace. No worries. I should tell the truth all the time. I got out of the study with its wood panelling and fascinating lino floor and ran to my bedroom to put my footy gear on.

When I came down, Mum and Dad were talking in the kitchen again. I think Dad was laughing, but he stuck his head in the fridge to look for something when I came in. He kept it in there for a while too, but finally pulled it out and a carton of eggs as well.

"Outside!" he said. I think I was wrong about him laughing. He was looking pretty serious now. I got the footy and headed for the back door.

"Leave the football," he said.

"But if we're gonna play footy, won't we need it?" I asked.

He gave me *the* look. I dropped the footy.

Dad followed me into the backyard, pointed to the fence and told me to stand in front of it. "Take your top off!" he barked.

"Why?"

"Take it off," he repeated. And I did. "Pull your shorts down at the back so your butt crack is sticking over the top."

"Why?"

179

"Father in heaven! Look, would you just stop asking questions and for once do what I say?" I did. Mum came over and gave me an ice-cream. It had already started melting so I went to lick it.

"Let it drip over your hand," said my father.

"Why?" I asked again.

"Ughhh!" grunted my father.

"Sorry." I was feeling like an idiot. I had no shirt on, my footy shorts were halfway down my bum and there was a perfectly good ice-cream melting in my hand.

"What are you thinking about?" asked my father.

"I don't know. I feel like an idiot," I said.

My father pulled his arm back and threw an egg at me. It went *splat* as it hit me smack-bang in the middle of the chest. And it hurt.

"Ow!" I bleated. There was egg and ice-cream all over me.

"Well, imagine how poor Nigel Humpy felt earlier this evening. DON'T THROW EGGS!!! In fact don't throw anything at anyone. EVER! Have a bath and go to bed," he said.

"Sorry," I said.

"Yeah," he almost smiled. "So am I. G'night, son."

"Night, Dad."
"Good shot, son."
"What, Dad?"
"Go to bed."

Trail Hunter

"You can do what I did: you can go out there and earn it. And I'll tell you something else, my little dahlingk, it's a lot easier to pull a penny out of a pauper now than it was in my day." That was my mother's reaction when I told her about the gleaming piece of chrome that practically winked at me from Mr Spokes' Cycle World window when I walked past that afternoon.

At $299.95, the Trail Hunter, with its chrome-molly chassis, blue handlebars, rims and cogs, tungsten goose neck, carbon graphite spokes and genuine knobby tyres, was nothing if not attractive. In fact, it was more than that. It left Belinda Douglas and her sway back a long way behind, and everyone knew that Belinda was the most beautiful thing in the seventh grade.

In fact, Belinda had to look out. There was a new beauty in town, and she had twenty-one gears.

Light and sleek, with clean lines, and she was obviously fast. Fast and ruthless. I couldn't imagine a gutter, a pothole or a pile of dirt that would be safe from the two of us together. The only thing the Trail Hunter was not, was mine. But I had a feeling that my mum could remedy that.

That's why I went to her and told her about the Trail Hunter, vision of my dreams, key to my good behaviour. I told her if she got me the bike then it was pretty much guaranteed that I would be good as often as possible.

"How about all of the time?" she asked me.

"Do I get the Trail Hunter?" I replied.

And that's when she hit me with the you-can-go-out-there-and-do-what-I-did-and-earn-it speech. It was disappointing. I was hoping at the very least that she would give me the we'll-see-what-your-father-says speech or even the your-birthday-and-Christmas-are-just-around-the-corner speech, but not this. Not you-can-go-out-and-earn-it.

This was a whole new speech I'd never heard before. I couldn't work out whether to laugh at it or cry. If I screamed and had a tantrum she might just give in, so I started to wobble my chin in anticipation of the impending riot. But she looked at me, half smiling, and stopped me before I could get started.

"For God's sake," she quipped, "don't even try that one. What are you, two? You're too old for a tantrum, and I think your father already told you only to cry when you break a bone, rip your skin or during a sad movie."

"C'mon, please Mum, pleeeeeaaaaaaaaaaa-sssssssssseeeeee?" I begged. "I'll do anything. I'll never ask for nothing ever again."

"Anything," she interrupted.

"That's what I said."

"No, you said 'nothing', but the word is 'anything'. You will never ask for anything."

"Okay, anything. I'll never ask for any-thing never, ever again. But I have to have that bike. Pleeeasse!!????"

And she hit me with it again. You-can-do-what-I-did-and-go-out-and-earn-it.

"What does that mean?" I asked her. "Earn it. What exactly does 'earn it' mean? What are you talking about, Mum?"

No emotional displays, no tantrums, no negotiations, nothing. I didn't know how I'd get the Trail Hunter and I wanted it more than anything I'd ever wanted before. More than

Big Jim's Hobie Cat, more than Silver, the Lone Ranger's Horse, my skateboard, Razor scooter, magic sets and boogie board. I wanted it more than I wanted my birthday to be every day of the year. And all I was hearing from my mother was "earn it".

"Earning it," she said, "was how I got my first bike. I got a job and earned the money so I could buy the bike myself. It was a beauty too. A REPCO, which, incidentally, does not stand for Recommended Every Part Comes Off, as your uncle used to say. It was purple, but not standard purple – it was purple with silver flecks and specks." Her eyes were starting to water and her face was turning red like it does when she's either really happy or really angry. Nah, she was happy; she had that dreamy look she gets when she looks at her wedding photos with Grandma.

"It had a sissy bar with a banana seat and reflectors on the mudguards. My dad, your grandfather, bought me a bell, and Mum, your grandma, gave me a big orange flag on the day we picked it up. She was beautiful, the most beautiful bike in the world." *Yeah*, I thought, *reflectors, bells, flags and mudguards – sounded really cool.*

"If it was good enough for me to go out there and earn a bike, then it'll be good enough for you. It was character-building, and I appreciated it more than I would have if the bike had been given to me, and that, Jack, is a fact."

She'd gone mad! She was using words I had never even heard of, and my name isn't Jack.

"What did you do?" I asked her. "How did you raise the money to buy your stupid bike?"

"Listen, Bugalugs, it wasn't a stupid bike and I worked very hard to get it, thanks very much for asking. I worked all kinds of jobs, even in a retirement home where I learned *respect for my elders*." She sounded annoyed.

"I'll ask Dad," I said. "He'll let me have it."

"Not this time, Smugsy. I'll make sure of that. Besides, your father worked his whole thirteenth summer just to buy himself the speargun he accidentally winged your grandmother with at Mount Martha. No, you'll have to earn it by plying your trade in the trenches, in amongst the working class, and getting those tender little mitts of yours soiled."

"Australian, Mum. Speak Australian. I don't

know what you're talking about."

"Okay, here's the deal. You will have to get a job, which means you do work and someone gives you money and when you have enough money, you buy your bike, not before. Okay?"

"But how? What do I do? Who will I work for?" I asked. "And isn't that what pocket money is?"

"You don't seriously think you *earn* your pocket money, do you?"

I didn't give her an answer. She didn't deserve one. Only I knew how hard I worked at pretending to help around the house. I didn't expect her to understand.

"Mow lawns, clean cars, paint letterboxes, weed gardens, I don't know, there are a million things you can do. You just need to use your grey matter, which is the stuff that keeps slopping around inside your head. And if you do that, you'll have your Trail Hurter in no time."

"Hunter, Mum, it's a Trail Hunter."

"Whatever," she said, and walked inside.

A job, get a job. What was with that? I decided to run away.

If they wouldn't give me the Trail Hunter,

then I wouldn't hang around. I'd leave, maybe find some parents who loved me enough to give me the things that would make me happy. Besides, once they realized the reason I ran away they would have to get me the bike, wouldn't they?

I began making plans immediately.

I wrote a note.

Bye, Mum and Dad, see you when I see you, if you don't see me first. Don't forget to feed my fish. I have run away and I won't be coming back for a very long time.

Fergus

I put some clothes into a bag, got some crisps from the pantry and a bottle of Fanta and headed for the door. I slammed it just to make sure they heard me go.

I headed straight for the pine trees. Well, they weren't actually pine trees; they're called conifers. They look like pine trees but with more leaves. They're kind of a bushy pine tree, and they're excellent for hiding in. I climbed the tree next to the one that had the cubby my dad had built. The first place they'd look for me would be the cubby. This way they'd never find me.

I found a perch that was well hidden *and* comfortable so I could watch the comings and goings of the house, which, for a Saturday afternoon, weren't many.

Dad got the mower out from the shed and swore a lot when he couldn't get it started, then he went inside and I didn't hear from anyone again until he started calling my name.

"Fergus… FERRRRRRRRR…GUSSSSSSSSSSS, you come out here right NOW!!!"

He sounded angry. He must have found the note.

"FERRRRRRRRRGUSSSSSSSSS!" hollered my mother. "FERRRRRRRRRGUSSSSSSSS! Where are yooooooooooooooooooooooooooooooooooooo-uuuuuuuuu????"

When my mother called me, she turned it into a kind of song. Almost like she was yodel-ling. I had often wished my name was Ted or Brad or Tim, because it's hard to yodel a short name.

"FERGUS??? FERRRRRRRGUS???" sang my mother. Dad was belting it out as well.

They came directly under the tree I was

sitting in and Dad looked up and yelled out, "Fergie Ferg, if you are in that cubby house you had better come out yesterday or you can kiss your pocket money and your toys goodbye. Do you hear me, Fergus? I mean it, and if I have to come up there and I find you, you'll know that trouble has a whole new name. Do you hear me??? Trouble will be spelled D-A-D! Fergus? Fergie Ferg?"

"He might not be up there. He might really have run away. He might be gone, dahlingk." My mother sounded worried, which was exactly what I was after.

"He's up there, dahlingk," said my father, teasing my mother and the way she said "darling". "And if he can hear me he better come down now, because he really doesn't want me to come and get him. Does he, Fergie Ferg???"

I didn't say a word, didn't budge. I saw him start lumbering up the tree next to me. He was huffing and puffing and cursing. And he wasn't at all happy when he poked his head through the door of the cubby and saw that I wasn't there.

I almost felt sorry for him, watching the colour drain from his face as he climbed down to Mum and gave her the news. "Not there," is all he said, but he looked pretty concerned.

"He's not there? So where is he if he's not there? He always hides up there. Doesn't he? Has he got a new hiding spot?" she asked.

"I dunno," said my father, conserving his words. The only thing he really wasted was butter, and he spread that on so thick you would've thought it was cheese. "I don't know where he is. Why has he run off, anyway? What did you do to him? You didn't hit him, did you?"

"How dare you!!!" she scolded him. "I have never... I would never. I simply said that he could go out and earn enough money to buy a Rail Hugger. I told him he can't expect us to give him everything, and that it's time he got some responsibility."

"Is the Rail Hugger a train or something?" he asked.

"No, it's a bike, and it's not that expensive – which is why he can go and earn it himself."

"Rail Hugger's a funny name for a bike. It's a better name for a train. How much is it anyway? I mean, if it's not that big a deal, maybe we should bite the bullet and give it to him as an early birthday present." My plan was working. This was the whole point of run-

194

ning away. Once Dad convinced Mum to give me the bike, I'd wait for them to go looking for me, then come down, cry a bit, apologize, maybe even tell them I loved them, and the Trail Hunter would be mine. I sat still and continued to watch.

"I don't think so, not this time. If we give him whatever he wants whenever he wants it, he'll just turn into a spoilt brat. As it is he has more toys than he knows what to do with. No, I'm sorry, dahlingk. He can earn it like I earned my first bike, my purple REPCO. The cool one."

"It's just that—" my father began to protest.

"It's just that nothing. I worked bloody hard to get my bike and I loved it because I earned it. And it was no picnic either..." Mum was getting worked up, which was not a good sign. When she lectured Dad she usually won, and not always because she was right. Sometimes I reckon he just gave in to get some peace and quiet. I thought about cutting my losses and falling out of the tree. That way at least they'd feel sorry for me and I wouldn't get into as much trouble for running away...

"I spent a whole summer working in that old folks' home," continued my mother. "A whole summer! I had to do all sorts of things: sweep and clean and wash. God, I even had to empty bedpans. I was thirteen." As Mum was getting more excited, Dad was backing off. "My first job was to clean their teeth. I thought that meant helping them with a toothbrush, but it didn't mean that at all.

"I had to go to them one at a time, take out their false teeth, dip them in some kind of acid that made them white, rinse them in mouthwash and put them back in their mouths.

"I tried a shortcut and collected the teeth from one whole ward, put them on a tray, cleaned them, all the time thinking how clever I was, and then, when it came time to put them back in the old folks' mouths, I couldn't remember whose teeth were whose." Dad started laughing. "It's not funny, Dugald. It took me hours to work out whose teeth belonged to who. It's impossible to talk or even eat with someone else's teeth in your mouth. It was terrible."

"What did you do?" giggled my father.

"I waited to see who didn't eat their lunch, then swapped their teeth around until everyone was smiling. It took hours, and I can tell you it wasn't funny. Not for me or anyone else. God, you can be insensitive, sometimes I wonder how I married you."

I covered my mouth and blocked my nose to stop myself from laughing. I thought my brains were going to blow out my ears. Dad started pulling weeds out of the ground. He looked like he was trying not to laugh.

"That's not the worst of it either," said my mother. My father looked like he was crying, he was laughing so hard. "One day Mrs Tittle asked me to help her get dressed. She was enormous, the size of a house, and she had huge breasts that looked like flattened watermelons when she was naked."

"You saw her naked?" asked my father.

"They don't bathe in their underpants, you idiot. Of course I saw her naked!" Mum barked. "I had to help her get them into her bra, so I tried to gently stuff them in bit by bit, and she abused me the whole time because I was hurting her. I wish I had never found her proper teeth.

"Finally she pushed me out of the way and

said, "You don't stuff them in like *that*. You do it like this." She then rolled up her bosoms one at a time like they were great big squashed sausages – no, they were more like big fat pancakes. She rolled up her pancakes and tucked them neatly into her bra. When she had them in a neat package, she said, 'Stop gawking, girl, and do me up at the back!'

"'Oh,' I said to her, 'that's how you do it.'

"'Yes,' she barked at me. 'And don't you forget it.' It was humiliating, Dugald. I won't even tell you how we got her underpants on."

My father was doubled over laughing. He was saying, "Tell me – tell me about the underpants—" He had tears pouring out his eyes and he was holding his stomach. It was too much for me as well. I let go of the tree to hold my mouth and my nose and I started to fall. I bounced from limb to limb and finally landed in a giggling heap between my mother and my father.

"Ow!" I said.

My dad stopped laughing, but only for a moment. I started up again once I realized I was all right, and Mum bellowed, "We'll just see how funny it is at the end of summer, won't we, mister smarty pants?! No bike for you unless you earn it, and no pocket money for worrying us by pretending to run away."

With that she stormed off. Dad and I sat on the ground laughing together. "Can I have the bike?" I asked him.

"No," he said, and he got up and followed Mum. "Tell me about Mrs Tittle's underpants," he yelled after her.

So I rang my grandfather. He gave me stuff all the time.

I told him about the Trail Hunter and how I needed to get $299.95. "Son, if you need something, you have to go out there and get it. Back in my day they used to give you a refund on lemonade bottles, so I used to steal the empties from our neighbours and cash those in at the corner store. I'm not saying you should do it, but it worked for me." *Yeah thanks, Grandpa*, I thought. *That was probably back in the days when people actually drank lemonade.*

In a word, I was stuffed. If I wanted the bike, I was going to have to earn it, and I hated the thought of that as much as I loved the thought of the Trail Hunter.

Dad said I was too young to work at

McDonalds, and besides, I didn't have the pimples. So it would have to be real work, and at Mum's suggestion, I plied my trade all over town. I travelled the neighbourhood, bucket and sponge in hand, washing every filthy car I could find. At five dollars a car it was slow work, but slow money was better than none at all.

I went to one house at ten o'clock in the morning. It was home to what had to be the filthiest car in the world. A man in his pyjamas answered the door. I asked him if he wanted his car washed for five dollars. He said okay, pointed me toward the hose and said, "Wake me when you finish." What a slug.

I washed and scrubbed and wiped and still it wouldn't come clean, but I did my best and when I couldn't do any more I knocked on the door and waited. No answer. So I knocked again, a bit louder and eventually he came to the door, still in his PJs.

He shuffled out, rubbing the sleep from his eyes, looked at the car, looked at me, looked back at the car and said, "It's still dirty. When you've cleaned it properly, wake me up again."

"But I can't get it off. The dirt's stuck. I've tried."

"Give us ya rag," he groaned, and tried to

get the sap and bird poo off himself. "Yeah, you're right. Doesn't come off, does it. I'll get ya money. What was it again? How much?"

"Five dollars."

He opened the car door and started ferreting round under the seats, in the ashtray and in the glove box. Eventually he tipped a pile of coins into my hand and said, "There you go, five bucks. I'm going back to bed, so don't bother me again. Okay?"

"Yeah, okay," I said. I was devastated. Deep down I knew that five dollars was five dollars, but it seemed so much more when it was in a note. He slammed the door as he went inside and I was so angry I could feel tears burning my eyes. I decided to get even with the slug and whizzed all over his door handles. It didn't make me any more money, but I felt better.

So I cleaned cars, mowed lawns, weeded gardens, cleaned windows, and even painted Mr Needlebottom's picket fence. I was relieved of that job after only a day, when the wind made paint blobs fly mysteriously off the fence and onto the cars parked nearby.

Mr Needlebottom was nice enough about it, but I did see him the next day scrubbing his

201

bumper clean. I would have done it for him for five dollars.

It was a tough summer, and I worked harder than I thought I could. Everyone in our street knew I was working to buy the Trail Hunter, and they were all pretty good at giving me jobs, though some were better than others.

I kept my money in a jar under my bed and counted it every single night. At first it didn't take me long, but as I earned more, the counting took longer, and I always found the time to do it.

Mrs Belfries' yard looked like a lawn now instead of the paddock of weeds it'd been before I started mowing it. Most of the cars in the street were clean most of the time and I seemed to get in less trouble at home, but maybe that's because I was hardly ever there. I hadn't turned into a complete suck: Mr Petrie's dogs still barked at me, probably because I kicked his front gate whenever I went past. I didn't hate his dogs, I didn't even hate him, I just loved getting the dogs jazzed up, knowing they had nowhere to go. He never walked them, so I suppose by getting the mongrels running around his yard yapping at me, I was doing him a favour. Maybe he should have paid me a fiver for that too.

I went past Mr Spokes' shop almost every day and there was the Trail Hunter, still in the window. There were others inside, of course, different colours with different options, but that was still my favourite.

I scrimped and saved. Mum decided to start giving me my pocket money again and slowly but surely I crept up on my target of $299.95. Eventually, after what seemed like forever, I had the money. All of it, stacks – and lots of it in notes. Two and a half jam jars full of plastic Australian money, the stuff that my grandpop says isn't really money because you can't burn it to light a cigar after a win at the races. He's a nutcase, of course.

The day I went to Mr Spokes' shop to buy the Trail Hunter, Mum and Dad came with me. They were kind of embarrassing, asking all the questions I already knew the answers to, and some I didn't care about. They asked about things like the warranty and safety features. Who cares about safety features? They even asked about a kickstand. I didn't want a kickstand; only losers had kickstands. How daggy did they want me to be? Besides, a kickstand would make the bike heavier, harder to table top and bunny hop, things like that. When they were satisfied, which was after quite a while, they told me to give the man the money.

My money, I thought. *Give the man my money.* And I did. I counted out the full $299.95, all those five-dollar notes, with a few kilos of shrapnel thrown in. It was beautiful; it made me smile. Mr Spokes didn't, though. He watched me like a hawk as I counted it all out, and when I'd finished, he counted it all out for himself. Dad said, "I'm sure it's fine." But Mr Spokes kept on counting.

"Plan for the divorce, not the marriage," he said. Mum, Dad and I all looked at each other wondering what he was on about.

"Must have been a lawyer in a previous life," whispered Dad.

"Just cautious," said Mr Spokes. Mum nudged Dad and he looked like he was blushing, but it was always hard to tell on weekends; he never shaved then.

When he'd finished counting, Mr Spokes nodded and put the money in the cash register. There was a fantastic *ding* when he closed it. "I love the *ding* of a good sale," he said.

"Mmmmmmmm, ding-a-ling-ding-ding," said Dad. Mum buried her elbow deep into his ribs this time. I don't think she was too impressed with Dad taking the mickey out of Mr Spokes. I didn't care; I was about to get my bike.

Mr Spokes pulled my Trail Hunter out of the window, adjusted the seat, tightened the pedals and greased the chain.

Dad plopped my helmet on my head and said, "We're proud of you, Fergus. See you at home."

And eventually they did.

ABOUT THE AUTHOR

Andrew Daddo is one of the sharpest new voices for young people. His first book, *Chewing the Seatbelt* – originally called *Sprung!* – became an instant bestseller when it was published in Australia, encouraging him to take pen to paper with a series of sequels and a threatened prequel (everybody's doing it). When he's not writing, Andrew is one of Australia's best known television personalities, presenting everything from music shows to holiday programmes. He lives on Sydney's northern beaches but will fish or play golf anywhere.